CLASH

Hard Hit 12

CHARITY PARKERSON

--Warning: This book is intended for readers over the age of 18.

Copyright © 2017 Charity Parkerson
Editor: Hercules Editing & Consultants
All rights reserved.
ISBN-13: 978-1-946099-25-9

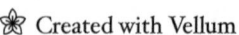

INTRODUCTION

Michael let Gavin keep him a secret once. Never again.

In high school, Michael and Gavin were total opposites. Michael was scholarly while Gavin was the athlete. Gavin chased all the girls and tormented Michael for being gay. Michael endured Gavin's public taunts with grace, because he knew the truth —he was the relationship Gavin really wanted. That is, until Gavin went too far and pushed Michael away for good.

It's been years since they've seen each other, but not much has changed. Gavin is still the athlete, playing for a minor-league hockey team. Michael still hates him. But fate loves a good laugh, and the pair end up stranded together during a flood. Things heat up fast, but can they survive more secrets or will Gavin finally destroy Michael for good?

AUTHOR NOTE

Hard Hit books 11 & 12, Guard *and* Clash, *have timelines that run concurrently. While Mara had things going on in her life, Michael was suffering his own drama. This is his story.*

CHAPTER ONE

A lifetime ago, when Michael first knew the bastard...

The party raged on inside the den. As usual, Michael didn't fit in. This was his brother's crowd. Marshall was the popular twin. Michael was the average one. He got good grades but was mediocre at sports. It was odd sometimes having an identical twin who really wasn't anything like him at all. Marshall was well-liked and everything he touched was golden. He was quarterback for the football team, played baseball and basketball. Michael had given up trying to measure up a long time ago. It didn't help that he was the gay twin of the most popular guy in school. Yeah, that sucked.

He could hear the crowd of loud teenagers, stamping from the den to the backyard and back again. Each time they passed his bedroom door, Michael tensed. It was one thing not to fit in at school. When it came home with him, it was worse. Michael focused on his video game, trying to tune out the noise. He should've known Marshall wouldn't let him hide all night.

His twin's green eyes and dark hair popped inside the room, focusing on Michael. "Come join us. We're about to hit the pool, and Chrissy just popped the lock on the liquor cabinet."

Marshall always tried to get Michael involved. The problem was Marshall was blind to how much his friends hated and bullied him. He was blind to a lot of things. "Nah. I'm good. Don't get drunk and drown."

"Come on, Micha—"

A large hand appeared through the crack in the door, smacking Marshall upside the head. "No homos allowed."

Marshall gave chase. "Fuck you, Gavin. Don't disrespect my baby brother."

Michael tried working up a smile. Marshall always defended him while pulling out that two-minute age difference. The smile wouldn't quite take because he could still hear the laughter in Marshall's voice as he chased Gavin down the hall. An ache started in the center of his chest. Of course it had been Gavin. At seventeen, Gavin Weeks was already over six feet of perfection. His dark hair always fell in his eyes, doing nothing to hide his intense almost amber gaze. He was the guy everyone wanted to be or do. Michael was no exception, even though Gavin was a complete ass.

Gavin: *Everyone is out back at the pool. Meet me in the driveway.*

He was also the ass Michael couldn't stay away from.

After shoving his phone in his back pocket, Michael quietly slipped outside, leaving through the front door to avoid the crowd. He could hear the shouts, laughter, music, and splashing coming from the backyard as he searched the dark for Gavin. A gasp escaped him as a pair of strong arms encircled him from behind. Michael went hard as Gavin's mouth opened over the side of his neck. Just like that, Michael was on fire. All the slurs against him in public slipped away when Gavin's mouth was on his skin. He already knew those hateful words would come roaring back the moment he was alone. That was the roller coaster he was stuck riding.

"Damn, I've been dreaming of you on your knees all night."

Oh, God. Gavin would make it worth his while. He always did. He'd been Marshall's best friend for years and stayed at their home countless times. It had only been six months since Gavin cornered Michael one night and stolen a kiss. He'd been sneaking into Michael's room ever since. They'd yet to have sex, but it wasn't for lack of Gavin trying. The problem was— Michael was already half in love with Gavin. If Gavin made love to him, Michael would be lost. What then? They'd never be a couple. Those slurs and insults Gavin hid behind were already destroying Michael. As Gavin spun Michael in his arms and their mouths met, he felt whole. He didn't understand how someone so wrong could feel so right while touching him.

Laughter moved closer and Gavin shoved him away. Michael barely finished scrambling for footing before Marshall, David, and Zoey rounded the corner. Michael nearly groaned. David especially loved tormenting him. He'd been taught hatred at his father's knee and loved telling Michael he was going to hell.

"What do we have here?" David said, sounding overly loud and drunk. "Have you been hiding in the dark, making out with the homo?"

"Don't," Marshall said, half-heartedly attempting to stop what Michael already knew would escalate into something awful.

"Shut your fucking mouth," Gavin growled, drawing all eyes his way. His hands were curled into fists and his face was set in a hard line. A bad feeling rose in Michael's gut. Everything felt wrong.

"Or what?" David said, taking a step in Gavin's direction. "People might find out the truth?" David added, still taunting Gavin. "Are you worried Marshall might find out how hot you've been for his dick? Since you know you can't have it, you turned to the lesser brother. At least you can get your dick sucked while staring down at identical eyes. Everyone already—"

David's head snapped back as Gavin's fist connected with the center of his face. A crunching sound rent the air, and hot blood streaked out, splashing Michael's arm. He couldn't move or speak. Horror kept him in check. He couldn't decide if it was David's claims or Gavin's violent reaction that shocked him more.

Michael's gaze shot to Marshall's. His face was a dark mask, making Michael's horror deepen. He believed David's claims. Michael knew his twin too well. He could see it written in every line of his brother's face. Without a word or waiting to see who won, Michael walked away. His Jeep was blocked in, but the vehicle was a place of solitude in a moment when he needed the world to be quiet. He jumped behind the wheel and shut himself inside. Michael couldn't stop himself from staring at the driver's side mirror, watching the action. David and Gavin rolled around on the ground. Marshall dragged out the hose and turned it on them. Michael couldn't hear what was said, but he heard the laughter when it began. Gavin scrambled to his feet and slung his arm over Zoey's shoulders, steering her away—like she was the prize for winning.

Michael couldn't breathe. David's claims wouldn't leave him. Was it true? Had Gavin turned to him because he couldn't have Marshall? He didn't know how long he sat there, letting the hurt and silence engulf him. Michael had done this to himself. He'd let Gavin keep him a secret.

A movement at the corner of his vision caught his eye. Michael turned his head, catching sight of Gavin and Zoey sneaking into the bushes, feet from where Gavin had kissed him earlier. A kernel of hatred sprang to life in his heart. Michael couldn't look away as Zoey kissed a path down Gavin's body, going down onto her knees. Something inside him broke. Michael started the Jeep, needing to get out of there. He didn't care if he had to hit another car to accomplish it. The instant Michael's Jeep fired to life, Gavin's head jerked up. His gaze fixed on the driver's side window. Michael knew it was too dark for Gavin to see him, but he knew Gavin understood he was busted. He didn't push Zoey away the way he had Michael. The kernel of hatred became an inferno of loathing. He would never, ever forgive Gavin for this.

The passenger side door opened and Marshall slipped inside. He didn't look Michael's way. "Let's go. Chris is moving his truck so you can get out."

Michael's eyes burned. Sometimes, he forgot how amazing his brother could be. He wanted to thank his twin for going with him, but his throat wouldn't work.

Still, Marshall stared straight ahead, not looking Michael's way. "I'll never forgive that fucker for this," Marshall said, sounding as furious as Michael felt.

Michael couldn't get his voice to work until they were halfway down the road, even then he only managed a whisper. He glanced Marshall's way. "Thank you for coming with me."

Marshall finally looked his way. "You'll always be my twin. Everyone else is replaceable."

He'd always wondered how much Marshall knew

but kept quiet. Even knowing he wasn't alone, Michael still couldn't talk about it. Maybe if he kept his mouth shut, no one would ever know how big of an idiot he'd been, but he'd know. Michael would never forget.

CHAPTER TWO

Present day, when the bastard returns to Michael's life...

The Steele household screamed old money. Luckily, Gavin was still in his element there. His father was third-generation professional athlete and his mom was a fourth-generation doctor. He'd always been a bit of a chameleon, fitting in wherever he went. Gavin played hockey for a minor league team and traveled all over the world. He'd been drunk in the seediest of bars and worn thirty-thousand-dollar suits in the grandest of clubs. Gavin had been and done everything in between, and none of it suited him. He'd given up caring a long time ago in favor of existing to the best of his abilities. Happiness was only a fairytale—a myth people spread, so they kept getting up every day.

Kieran and Henley Steele made happiness look real, though. It was depressing. Gavin was kicking himself for having to disturb them today. He'd scheduled ice time with Henley at a local rink, but given the couple's state of undress and the dark looks Kieran kept tossing his way, neither man had been prepared for Gavin to show up on time.

"Sorry if I came too soon," Gavin said for the third time. He just wanted to get out of there intact. Unfortunately, Henley still had to get his shoes on.

A low knock landed on the door, saving Gavin from groveling. At least he wasn't the only person bent on breaking up the pair today. He was ready for someone else to be the center of Kieran's rage-filled attention.

"Come," Kieran barked, not bothering to hide his irritation. A man with dark hair dipped inside Kieran's office, carrying a bottle of wine. Gavin's heart stopped. He didn't need a moment to adjust or rack his brain for where he'd seen the man before. Gavin would know him anywhere.

"Am I disturbing you? Your maid said I'd find you in here."

Goddamn. Gavin's stomach muscles tightened. That sexy voice—it had haunted his memories. His dreams. The man's gorgeous green gaze slid his way.

"Sorry again, Gavin," Henley said behind Gavin.

"No problem," Gavin mumbled, hoping that was the right response, since he'd lost the ability to think straight the moment Michael Frost stepped into the room.

"It's not like me to be late."

Gavin didn't respond to Henley's claim. The ice in Michael's gaze as he stared at Gavin held Gavin hostage.

Kieran said something to Michael, even going as far as to snap his fingers to get Michael's attention. Michael turned his face away, focusing on Kieran. Gavin wanted to cry out in denial at the loss. Words were exchanged. Gavin heard none of it. Sound was lost to him. All Gavin cared about was watching Michael's lips move. It had been six long years since they'd held each other's stare. Michael's gaze moved back his way, as if he was as incapable of looking away from Gavin as Gavin was him. Michael said something else to Kieran and then headed for the door. He was leaving. Gavin couldn't let him get away.

He spoke over his shoulder to Henley as he chased after Michael. "I'll wait outside for you, Hen, and let you say your goodbyes." Luckily, Henley didn't argue, because Gavin only had one thing on his mind —forcing Michael to acknowledge him.

He waited until they were outside before calling out to stop Michael. "Michael, hold up. Are you going to run away without saying hi?"

Michael slowed next to a red Mercedes. When he turned, there wasn't an ounce of emotion on his gorgeous face. Those green eyes of his, fuck. It was like getting punched in the gut.

"I'm not running away. I have a schedule to keep, but hi."

Gavin couldn't fight the smile tugging at his lips. They hadn't spoken in years. It seemed he hadn't been missed. Michael wasn't one to pretend. In fact, that was one of the reasons Gavin hadn't been able to resist him. "How have you been?"

Michael didn't soften at all. "Good."

"What about your family?" Gavin pressed, refusing to give up.

"If you're fishing for information about Marshall, he's fine. I'm sure he'd love to hear from you. If you don't mind, I'm expected elsewhere."

Gavin's smile fell. "We both know Marshall wouldn't care to hear from me. Nor do I care to speak to him. I was merely making conversation with you."

"I thought we both knew I don't care to hear from you either, yet here we are."

There it was—Michael's hatred. Gavin shoved his hands in his pockets and fought the urge to squirm beneath Michael's open loathing. "I was a scared teenager, Mikey," Gavin said, intentionally using the pet name only he'd been allowed to use.

A hint of something unnamed flashed in Michael's eyes. His shoulders seemed to relax a hair, but none of the hardness left his voice. "Are you a scared adult?"

Gavin held Michael's gaze. "No."

"Then you should go see my brother," Michael said, the first sliver of emotion peeking though. Gavin heard the slight crack in Michael's words, as if the suggestion physically hurt.

"Hey, Gavin. I'm going to wait in the car, okay?"

Gavin glanced over his shoulder at Henley's words. "It's unlocked." By the time he turned his attention back Michael's way, he'd slipped inside his car and was backing away. Gavin watched him leave. He didn't chase after him this time, but he still made his confession as if Michael could hear him. "I don't want Marshall. Never have."

———

They had mutual friends. Fuck his life. Michael hadn't even seen it coming. It had been six glorious years since he'd set eyes on Gavin Weeks. Gavin fucking Weeks. Michael could barely think his name. The sick and twisted hatred dug its claws into Michael's gut anew—like everything happened yesterday rather than years ago. His boss, Mara, sent him to deliver a bottle of wine to one of her friends before meeting her on set. That was it. It was that simple. Like that—fucking Gavin Weeks had been staring at him from across the room. He had the same almost-amber eyes. The same dark hair that couldn't be tamed. He was wider—like his shoulders had filled out. To his shame, the muscles in Michael's stomach had tightened with the same instant longing he'd always experienced when looking at Gavin. If it weren't for Gavin, Michael wouldn't have known it was possible to hate someone and still want to fuck them. He stared at his phone, sightless. All he saw or heard was the memory of Gavin. He'd let Gavin change him. Shape him into someone bitter and closed. It seemed he really never would forgive the man. He didn't know how.

Without realizing it, Michael found himself absorbed by the scene Mara worked on. She was such an amazing actress, sometimes he forgot where he was. Her words washed over him, sucking him in, and drawing his gaze toward one of the screens showing the scene. Mara stared at a spot where the camera could get a close-up and spoke as if her co-star stood there rather than a cold piece of equipment. "I still remember the day I realized we were really over. For the life of me, I can't remember what you said or did, but I remember the way I felt the exact moment I realized you weren't mine any longer—the quiet acceptance that overcame me. My heart numbed. Losing you wasn't the saddest part of losing you. Losing me was the saddest part because I never recovered."

Goddamn. Wasn't that the truth?

"What are you playing? I always see you on this same game but haven't asked what it is."

Michael looked over at Cal's question. Thoughts of Gavin disappeared. As Mara's bodyguard, Cal had a lot of free time to hang around the set waiting—like Michael did every day. Michael flashed the phone he'd forgotten in his hand Cal's way. "It's called Cyborgs vs. Androids. You join a side, and then a team of other online players. You have to make it through levels and gather certain supplies to survive, as well as creating your own planet etc. It's pretty mind numbing, but it gives me something to do."

Cal nodded. "I guess you have to find ways to entertain yourself. Since I haven't been working for Mara long, I'm still enjoying the people watching. How long have you been doing this? Working for Mara, I mean?"

"Four years," Michael said, willing to talk if Cal was bored. Anything was better than thinking about his morning. Cal wasn't much of a talker. Michael was curious about the man, but not enough to ask questions. "I'm lucky. Mara is easy to keep up with and to please. Some handlers have miserable tasks. Look at Penny over there," Michael said, nodding toward a mousy-looking brown-haired girl on the other side of the room. "She's Ven Sterling's handler. The guy who's playing opposite of Mara," Michael explained, in case Cal didn't know who Ven was. "That guy is constantly pulling shit to get out of being where he's supposed to be. If you need entertainment, just watch. She spends half her day trying to find him. It's like her life is one big game of Hide and Seek. Meanwhile, Ven has got some set worker cornered in the backlot about half a second away from landing a sexual assault charge. Well, if he wasn't famous," Michael added, because the man would already be in jail if women weren't star struck by him.

"Huh," Cal grunted, which could've meant anything at all. "Why doesn't she quit?"

A snort escaped Michael before he could call it back. "Are you kidding me? She makes three times what Ven's body double makes, and she can come to work looking however she wants. Anyone can put up with anything for enough money."

Michael's phone chirped, alerting him to an incoming game message from one of his Cyborg team members. He gave up on his conversation with Cal and glanced at his phone.

#1HatTrick: *I have an extra cylinder of nanos and a diamond-infused exoskeleton, if you need them.*

MichaelThePA: *Hey. How are you? I have more nanos than I can use right now, but thank you for the new exoskeleton.*

#1HatTrick: *No problem. I'm good. How was your date last night?*

MichaelThePA: *Work ran late, so I didn't go. What did you do last night and how was your trip to Boston?*

#1HatTrick: *Lasagna for one, and I didn't close the deal.*

MichaelThePA: *Yum, lasagna. My favorite. I'm sorry you didn't win this one.*

#1HatTrick: *There's only me, so I'll be eating it for a few days. Don't worry over me. I always come out on top, and I have another trip Thursday to Winnipeg.*

MichaelThePA: *Think of me while you do. Eat, that is...*

#1HatTrick: *I will.*

Michael smiled as he read through their messages. He didn't even know the guy. They'd developed a friendship when they'd landed on the same team, but Michael didn't know much about him. He thought the man was some sort of corporate negotiator who traveled constantly. But, hell, Michael didn't even know his name much less was he sure exactly what he did for a living. Michael's smile fell. How sad was his life? Most people would kill for Michael's job, working as a PA and handler for Mara King, one of Hollywood's biggest actresses. He couldn't deny he had an awesome career. Everything else was a dead zone. He never saw his family. Michael had been single for always, and free time was a joke. Mara had confided months ago that she was considering retiring. If she did, his job would stand, but he'd have more time for a life of his own. Michael had no clue what he'd do then. There was only so much Cyborgs vs. Androids he could play.

"I need a favor," Mara said, interrupting his depressing thoughts. What Mara meant was—she needed him to do his job, but she was too nice to say as much.

He put his phone away. "Anything."

Her dark eyes shone bright with happiness—something he hadn't seen in a while. "Noah is in town. I had dinner with Troy and him last night, and I think I left my favorite red jacket in their hotel room. Could you head over there and pick it up for me?"

"Of course. Just text me the address of where I need to go."

Mara nodded. "Sure thing. Also, we're done for the day here, so once you've got it, you're free to go home. You can bring the jacket by tomorrow when you come in. No need for a special trip."

"Sounds good," Michael said, already heading for the door. He cast a quick glance Cal's way, ensuring he would take care of Mara from here on out. He already knew the man would, but it was Michael's job to make sure Mara got handed off to the next person in charge of her well-being. Michael took that job seriously.

Despite the fact that he had nothing to do, Michael looked forward to getting home earlier than usual. It wasn't often he could strip down to his boxer briefs and do absolutely nothing but relax. Unfortunately, at the hotel, Noah's husband Troy rerouted him to the municipal rink where Noah was out practicing with some local players.

"Sorry, man," Troy said for the third time. "Noah

planned to take it by her house after practice, so it's in his truck."

"It's fine," Michael reassured him. "She's not staying at her place right now, so I'll run by there and pick it up. Just let Noah know I'm on my way."

While holding in an irritated sigh, Michael waved over his shoulder as he headed for the elevator. Fuck. The local public rink was on the other side of town and it was rush hour traffic. Michael stared straight ahead and tried not to think as he inched down the highway. No matter how hard he fought against it, Gavin's image kept floating through his mind. He hadn't changed much in looks. Had he changed in personality? Michael doubted it. He didn't want to be bitter, but fuck. Gavin had built him up and torn him down too many times. The sick, defeated feeling Gavin left him with years ago had never gone away. Each time he thought of the man, he remembered how it felt to watch him with someone else. There were other memories too. Things he couldn't shake. The New Orleans heat beat down on the pavement, causing a haze in the distance. Michael stared at the waves of light floating through the air and let the memory of the first time they'd kissed take hold.

"Your house is the strangest one I've ever been in. There's never any adults here, and the fridge is always empty." It

was true; both Michael's parents were high-dollar lawyers and partners in the same practice. They were never home.

"But there's always money on the fridge, so we don't starve, and we have the best parties," Marshall said, snatching a fifty off the refrigerator door. "Want to run to the store with me to pick up snacks?"

Gavin grabbed a bottle of water from the fridge and twisted off the cap. "Nah. I think I'm gonna be lazy for a few."

"You're always lazy," Marshall said, attempting to put Gavin in a headlock.

Michael listened to the whole thing while leaning over the kitchen counter, trying to finish his calculus homework.

After much scuffling, Marshall ruffled Gavin's hair and headed for the door. "I'll be back in a few."

Gavin tossed the plastic cap from his bottle at Marshall's back. "I'll be here."

The back door closed and silence fell in the kitchen. It was uncomfortable. Five minutes passed. Gavin didn't leave. Michael focused harder on his work.

Gavin leaned over his shoulder. "What are you working on?"

"I'm not in the mood for your bullying bullshit today," Michael said, using his driest tone.

"What are you in the mood for?"

At Gavin's tone, Michael straightened and turned. Damned if Gavin didn't sound turned on. That was fucked up and couldn't be real. He had to see for himself. The instant he turned, Gavin's body collided with his. Michael was too shocked to move away. Gavin's erection dug into Michael's side. His gorgeous amber gaze stared down at Michael with hunger.

"Um, what's going on?" Michael's brain couldn't come to terms with what his eyes were seeing.

"This," Gavin said, dropping his head and touching his lips to Michael's.

Michael didn't react immediately. His first thought was to push Gavin away. This had to be a joke, except it didn't feel the least bit funny or fake. Then, Gavin sucked Michael's bottom lip between his teeth. Lust slammed into Michael, nearly doubling him over in its intensity. As if sensing his weakness, Gavin attacked. His hard body went flush against Michael. Their tongues brushed.

Soon, Michael would have to deal with the fact that Gavin Weeks was kissing him. Right now, all he wanted was for Gavin not to stop. Holy hell. It was explosive.

"Goddamn, I knew you'd be amazing," Gavin said as he changed angles.

Gavin said he knew as if he'd been thinking about this. Michael snapped. "Wait," he said, shoving at Gavin's chest. "Just wait." Gavin's eyes were heavy with lust. His lips were swollen from their kisses. Michael had never been more confused or turned on in his life. "I don't understand," Michael said, because he had nothing else.

"We've got maybe fifteen minutes before Marshall gets back. Do you want to talk about this now, or I can text you later?"

"I want to talk about this now," Michael said, because he was no fool. There had to be more to this than he currently understood, and he wouldn't risk Gavin refusing to answer him later.

"Okay. I want you."

Michael blinked. It was almost funny. Gavin made the claim loud and clear as if there wasn't a doubt inside him. This wasn't some random thing, or a joke. Gavin wanted him. "Text me later," Michael said, pulling Gavin back in for another kiss. This was nuts, but damn. Gavin was sexy as hell. Only an idiot would turn him down.

The honking of a horn behind him pulled Michael from his thoughts. He eased forward the five feet the driver behind him was angry over. It took everything inside him not to flip the guy off. As irritating as it was to have someone blow their horn at him that person wasn't who Michael was pissed off at. He was angry with himself. It had been six fucking years. He should be over this shit. It seemed stupid not to be. He would do better. If he saw Gavin again, Michael wouldn't let the man get under his skin. No one man was worth the hole in Michael's chest.

———

"No fucking way," Gavin said under his breath when he caught sight of Michael in the parking lot of the municipal rink. Twice in one day was more than a coincidence. It was a fucking miracle. "Michael," he shouted before the man could get away. The way Michael's shoulders immediately tensed and then fell at the sound of Gavin's voice made Gavin chuckle. It sounded evil even to his ears. He half expected Michael to make a run for it to keep from talking to him again. To Gavin's surprise, he turned, looking slightly put out.

"Are you stalking me?"

He was, but that was a different story. "I'm leaving practice." Michael's expression never changed, and it occurred to him that Michael didn't know him any longer. "I play for the Blue Fires." Still, Michael's expression didn't change. "It's a minor-league hockey team," he clarified.

"I'm aware," Michael said without a hint of emotion and leaving Gavin wondering which part he'd known.

"You ran away earlier." Gavin didn't know why he went there. He didn't like dancing around.

"I told you I had a schedule to keep." Michael's expression and voice never wavered from cool indifference.

Gavin shifted his workout bag to the other hand, giving his right arm a break. "And now?"

"Now I'm headed home. Have a good night."

Before Michael could run away again, Gavin grabbed his arm, stopping him. "Have coffee with me."

Michael's gaze dropped to where Gavin held him before he slowly lifted his chin and met Gavin's stare. The coldness in his eyes had Gavin releasing him. "It's seven at night."

"Dinner then," Gavin offered. "Or even just a drink. Twenty minutes of your time," Gavin tacked on, hoping Michael would give a little.

Michael glanced around the parking lot as if he was lost. Gavin didn't know if Michael would run or rage, but he didn't look likely to accept Gavin's offer.

He finally focused on Gavin. Gavin's stomach muscles tightened. He loved Michael's eyes. Time hadn't changed a thing. "Didn't there used to be a small bar around here? They served wings and whatnot."

Gavin had to bite his bottom lip to keep from giving in to a triumphant smile. "Sammie's. It's at the edge of the North parking lot. This is the South lot. I'll drive if that's where you'd like to go."

Michael tossed a jacket inside his Mercedes. "We're right here. You can ride with me. I mean, this is my company car, but my boss doesn't care what I use it for as long as I show up to work."

Since there was no way he would let Michael get away again, Gavin circled the car to the passenger's side and jumped in. He turned in his seat and set his bag in the back before buckling up. He waited until he was settled before glancing Michael's way again. The man was doing his best not to look Gavin's way. Gavin could see it in the way he remained tensed as if prepared to flee.

"This is a nice company car," Gavin said, hoping to break the tension. "I thought you'd planned to go to law school."

Michael put the car in drive. "I worked at my parents' law firm for a little over a year after high school, pushing papers and answering phones while I went to college," Michael said as he circled the large lot, heading for the North side. "It was awful. Everyone was angry and overworked. Then, one day, I met my boss when she came in to go over a contract. It was love at first sight, and she offered me a job. I quit college and went to work for her."

Gavin loved listening to Michael speak, so he kept pressing. "What do you do?"

Michael hesitated, as if he didn't want to say, before finally answering, "I'm Mara King's personal assistant and handler."

"Mara King. Like, the Mara King?"

A hint of a smile touched Michael's lips before disappearing again. Like that, Gavin knew Michael was proud of what he did. "I figured school would always be there if I wanted to go back. Being offered this job was a once in a lifetime opportunity I couldn't let pass. I haven't regretted it." He tossed a glance Gavin's way. "What about you? I thought football was your thing. How did you end up playing hockey?"

Gavin shrugged, even though Michael wasn't looking at him. "I was never very good at football. It's tough being the son of a famous quarterback turned coach. Everyone expected me to be the same, but I wasn't even good enough to warrant a scholarship. I went on to college anyhow, thinking I needed to do something with my life. They had skate-on tryouts for the university hockey team, and I'd played a little when I was a kid, so I gave it a shot. Turns out, I'm better at this." Since they were at the restaurant, it seemed ridiculous to stay in the car, so Gavin opened the door and kept talking. "Getting picked up by the Blue Fires has saved my dad's pride, a bit."

"Your parents were always proud of everything you did," Michael argued, proving he never knew them beyond the face they showed the public.

"Not so much anymore," Gavin said, hoping he could leave it at that.

Catching up carried them through dinner until the waitress dropped their check at the table and told them to pay the cashier. Gavin never looked the woman's way. He couldn't take his eyes off Michael. The man's every reaction screamed loathing. It was obvious Michael didn't want to be there, but he didn't leave. Gavin swallowed another large gulp of water, trying to fight back the urge to say all the things he really wanted to say. Michael stared at his own glass, stirring the ice with his straw. There was a deep line between his brows, and Gavin broke. He set his drink aside. Gavin couldn't take Michael's cool indifference any longer. "Why do you still hate me? I know I fucked up, but it's been years, and I'm trying here."

Michael stared at his hands as he toyed with the straw in his glass. He stayed silent for so long, Gavin wasn't sure he'd answer. His gaze lifted to Gavin's, and Gavin stopped breathing. He thought he hadn't forgotten a single detail of Michael, but the impact of his intensity had been lost to him until now. He'd forgotten how it felt to be underneath Michael's piercing green gaze.

"I hate you for the skip in my heart each time I remember you pushing me away." It was a punch to the gut. Michael didn't stop. "Every time in my life

I've wondered if I'm good enough can be traced back to you. I shouldn't care about those things any longer, but I do. It's not fair, but I hate that a single good thing has ever happened to you. You should question yourself. Your brain should be the same roller coaster. People should call you names and make your life hell if there was any justice in the world. But it seems you've continued on, living the same charmed life."

"My life was never charmed," Gavin admitted. "The only time I was ever free was when I was with you, and then it was temporary—always rushed so my fantasy of being me wasn't exposed to my reality. When I look back on the night I pushed you away, it's more than a skip in heartbeat. It's a knot in my stomach and fire in my throat." Gavin shook his head, trying to shake off the memory of losing Michael. A bitter smile touched his lips. "I see I'll never change your mind about me. Are you ready to go?"

Michael didn't budge. "Do you want to change my mind about you?"

"I don't know," Gavin lied.

"Then, yes. I'm ready to go," Michael said with a nod and stood. He grabbed the check before Gavin could get to it and was headed to the register without a backward glance. Gavin wanted to argue, but he couldn't stop staring at Michael's ass. His chest ached. There were tons of gorgeous men in the world. Gavin traveled all over for games. He could meet someone else, but Michael was the one who wouldn't leave his head. He'd seen Gavin at his worst and hadn't backed down until Gavin had tossed him away. Yes, he wanted Michael to change his mind about him. That was something that couldn't be forced. Gavin wasn't giving up.

CHAPTER THREE

*B*eing nervous wasn't a new state for Gavin. He was a wreck every time he stepped out onto the ice in front of thousands of fans. This was different. Whereas Michael might've punched him in the balls and spit in his face at seeing him again, Marshall was just as likely to kill him. Gavin wasn't sure which of the twins it was more painful to see, but if he wanted to win back the one he wanted, he'd have to apologize to both. Damn, every time he thought of Michael, his entire body tightened with desire. It was more than lust. He'd never stopped feeling like—wherever Michael was— he belonged to him. But the way Michael had looked at dinner—skinny jeans and tight Henley. Fuck. He was still sexier than any man Gavin had ever met.

More than anything, it was Michael's eyes. Gavin had never seen anyone else have the exact green that Michael did. Those eyes were gorgeous and mesmerizing. They'd always seen into Gavin's soul. There was nothing he wouldn't do for one more shot, including this.

Even though it was October, it was a typical New Orleans day. The sun shone brightly and boiled the air to eighty-five degrees. He'd called ahead, letting his dad know he was coming, so getting entrance into the Land Sharks' stadium wasn't an issue. There were a few people in the stands, watching practice. Gavin headed straight for the field. Having a father as the coach of a pro football team had its perks. In this case, it made it hard for Marshall to avoid him.

Everyone called Gavin's dad Coach, even his kids and wife. Most people had parents. Gavin had a man who directed players on a field. The man's dark blonde hair seemed lighter in the sunlight with his head bent over a dry-erase board. Almost as if he sensed Gavin's presence, his dad's head lifted, and his amber gaze moved Gavin's way.

The man smiled like the cameras were watching. "Hey, son. I see you made it inside okay."

"Yes, sir," Gavin said, moving to stand at his side. He eyed the players on the field. "How are you feeling about this year's lineup?"

Mimicking his pose, his dad's gaze moved over the men running plays. "I'm always optimistic. Marshall has stepped up well with our starter out."

Gavin nodded, hoping he didn't throw up. Marshall was the son his father should've had. "I knew he would."

"What made you decide to come by today?" his dad asked, obviously done with the small talk.

"Thought I'd see how you're doing and wish Marshall good luck." It was the best Gavin could come up with. Coach wasn't involved enough in Gavin's life to know Marshall hated him these days. He'd hated him ever since the night Gavin's life had fallen apart.

"You've got a lot of fucking nerve, hanging around here until I got back."

Goddamn. Gavin's head swam. He didn't know what to do or say. Marshall had forgiven him for a lot of shit over the years, but it didn't look like this would be one of those things. "I wanted to explain."

"Explain what?" Marshall growled. "I'm not stupid or blind, Gavin. All your stories about how you couldn't sleep and ran to the store—bullshit. Twice I saw you leaving his bedroom, but I said nothing. Every time you look at him, it's in your eyes. He's my brother."

"I know," Gavin said, hearing the defeat in his voice.

"Was David right?"

Gavin scrubbed his hands through his hair, trying to hold his shit together. "You know me better than anyone. David doesn't know me."

There was so much anger and hurt in Marshall's eyes. Gavin hated himself even more, and he hadn't thought that was possible. "I'm trying to be different. Goddamn it. I don't want to hurt anyone. Instead, I'm hurting everyone." Especially himself, and Gavin couldn't take it any longer.

"Don't come back here, Gavin. There's nothing left for you here."

"He's about to come off the field for the day," Coach said, pulling Gavin from the memory of the last time he'd spoken to Marshall. As if making good on his word, Coach blew his whistle and waved Marshall in. Marshall pulled off his helmet as he jogged their way.

His familiar green gaze slid Gavin's way. He might be Michael's twin, but Marshall's eyes weren't an exact match. Gavin knew the difference. "Hey, man. What's up?" Without waiting for Gavin to answer, he focused on Coach. "What's next?"

"That's it for the day."

Marshall nodded and switched his focus Gavin's way. "It's been a while."

Gavin smiled. His chest hurt. "You've been busy getting famous." Marshall flashed him a bright smile but didn't respond. Marshall had always been the humble sort. Gavin moved out of earshot of his dad, and Marshall followed. He didn't waste time coming to the point. Marshall didn't want him around. Not really, and Gavin didn't want to be there. "Two things, and I'll leave you in peace. I know it's too little too late, but I wanted to apologize for everything."

Marshall nodded. His good humor never faded. He was the personable twin. Funny how that had always been a turn off for Gavin. He liked Michael's deep intensity—the passionate twin. "It's been years, Gavin. No one cares about high school shit anymore."

Even though that wasn't remotely true, Gavin still breathed a sigh of relief. "It's good you feel that way, because I need Michael's number." There were easier ways he could've gotten it, but he needed to deal with Marshall.

Marshall's smile brightened, as if he relished the moment. "No."

He'd expected as much. "Okay. It was good seeing you again." Gavin moved to walk away.

Marshall spoke up, stopping him. "That's it? I tell you no, and you accept my answer? You don't deserve him because you've never had any desire to fight for him."

Confusion kept Gavin frozen in place. His brow

furrowed. "It's not like I can beat his number out of you."

"You could try," Marshall shot back.

"Michael and I have mutual friends. I can get it from one of them. The only reason I came here first is because Michael said I should come see you, and I realized I've never apologized. I hoped to kill two birds with one stone, but I'll go elsewhere."

"Wait," Marshall said, sounding confused. "You talked to Michael?"

Gavin nodded. "We had dinner last night."

"Oh." All humor was gone from Marshall's expression. So much for high school shit not meaning anything.

"He's always been the one, Marsh. I know you don't understand." Gavin moved to walk away again.

Marshall called out, stopping him. "His number is the same as it's always been. He's never changed it."

The smile tugging at the corners of Gavin's mouth was out of his control. "You won't be sorry, and for the record, my number is the same too."

Marshall shook his head, confirming Gavin's thoughts he'd never call. "I'm already sorry, by the way," he yelled at Gavin's back.

Gavin turned and walked backward, heading for the tunnel. "Don't worry. I won't tell him we spoke."

"You don't know him anymore," Marshall said, trying for one more dig.

"And you've never really known me," Gavin said with a shrug. "None of that changes a thing."

With a shake of his head, Marshall turned his back on Gavin, freeing him from this nightmare. Gavin jogged for the tunnel. His phone burned a hole in his pocket. Michael's number was still programed there. He was one step closer to heaven.

———

#1HatTrick: *What did you do last night?*

MichaelThePA: *Hey. How are you? I had dinner with a guy I used to know.*

#1HatTrick: *I'm good. Someone you used to know? How did that go?*

MichaelThePA: *He was my twin's best friend. I'm not sure how it went, to be honest. What did you do?*

#1HatTrick: *I sense a story. Spent some time working out with friends.*

MichaelThePA: *Too long of a story to tell. Did you have fun?*

#1HatTrick: *I suppose. If you want to tell your long story, I have time.*

MichaelThePA: *Maybe I should've said it's too painful of a story to tell.*

#1HatTrick: *So it's like that?*

MichaelThePA: *Yeah, it was. Really, though, I blame myself. I knew he was a dick before I let him get under my skin. It won't happen again.*

#1HatTrick: *How long ago was this?*

MichaelThePA: *6 years.*

#1HatTrick: *People change.*

MichaelThePA: *Maybe. Have you gotten any supplies for our camp?*

———

Gavin: *Don't ask how I knew your number is the same.*

Michael: *I see yours is too. How did you find out my number is the same?*

Gavin: *I said not to ask.*

Michael: *You're not the boss of me.*

Gavin: *Damn, you still make me smile. Have lunch with me.*

Michael: *Why?*

Gavin: *Because I'm hungry.*

Michael: *No. Why do you want to have lunch with me?*

Gavin: *Because I hate you too.*

Michael: *When and where?*

Gavin: *I'll pick you up.*

———

"You still have the old Jeep," Gavin said the moment Michael let him inside. Michael hated the way his stomach muscles tightened and butterflies stirred the instant he set eyes on Gavin. The man's tight black t-shirt and worn jeans did nothing to help matters.

"Yeah, it's still in good shape and there's no nicer vehicle than a paid for vehicle."

"You always were the smart one," Gavin said. "I wish it would've rubbed off on me. The SUV I'm driving now is nowhere near being paid off, and I probably won't keep it that long."

"Why am I not surprised you get bored with things quickly?"

A line appeared between Gavin's eyes as if confused by Michael's question. "No. It's a gas guzzler."

A hint of guilt wormed its way in. He shouldn't have agreed to this date if he planned to be a dick for every second of it. Michael tried to do better. "Would you like for me to drive, then?"

"Nope," Gavin said, sounding happy again. "It just struck me as odd to see the old Jeep sitting in the driveway of this house, because this is one hell of a house. Plus, I invited you. Are you ready? I need to stop and fill up first, but I have a plan."

A surprise? Michael had to fight to hide his smile. Nothing exciting ever happened to him. The smallest hint of something different had him moving. He moved for the door and Gavin followed, eyeing everything they passed, as if he still couldn't wrap his mind around the luxury. "I can't take credit for the house," Michael said as he pulled the front door closed behind them. He loved his beautiful home in the middle of nowhere. It was quiet and beyond anything he'd ever dreamed of having, but he didn't own it. "It's another part of my incentive package from Mara. She pays the rent."

"This is a fucking rental?" Gavin asked, sounding slightly horrified. "Jesus. This easily a million-dollar house. That's a hell of an incentive package."

"Mara is one hell of a lady," Michael said, incapable of hiding his pride. Maybe he didn't have Gavin, but life hadn't been a complete loss.

Gavin rushed ahead of him and opened the passenger side door of a dark-blue Escalade. A smile that felt shy, even to him, touched Michael's lips as he climbed in and Gavin closed the door behind him. As he buckled his seat belt, Michael caught sight of a sketch pad on the back seat. He thought he remembered everything about Gavin, but he'd forgotten how Gavin never went anywhere without art supplies. Even as a teenager, Gavin had possessed immense talent. Curiosity was killing Michael. He wanted to skim through every page and see how much Gavin had grown. Michael made it as far as the gas station before breaking. While Gavin pumped the gas, Michael snatched up the pad and flipped it open. The first drawing was an elf, carrying a bow and draped in long robes. Something about it looked vaguely familiar, but Michael couldn't place where he'd seen the drawing before. The next was a landscape of snowcapped mountains. It was so detailed Michael swore he could feel the chill in the air.

The door opened and Gavin slid behind the wheel. If he was the least bit put out by Michael going through his personal belongings, he didn't show it, nor did he try to stop Michael. "You're doing a lot of fantasy-themed drawings and people nowadays. It used to be mostly objects."

"I like the way people's expressions change. It's challenging to try to capture emotion. Plus, it gives me something to do with my time," Gavin said, sounding as if it wasn't important.

Michael glanced over and caught a certain glint in Gavin's eyes before he masked his thoughts. It didn't matter what Gavin said—it mattered. Michael didn't hide how impressed he was. "These are amazing. Truly. I'm sure you're good at hockey, but I wish you were doing something with this instead. You should be sharing this with the world. I always thought you'd be happier in the art field."

Gavin looked away, stealing Michael's shot at seeing Gavin's reaction to his words. "Art is just a hobby. No one will pay me to draw."

That was Gavin's dad talking. Michael recognized the tone. "You could've been an art teacher or a designer."

Gavin flashed him a sweet smile as he fired the SUV to life. "It's okay. I like what I do, and it might've killed my love for drawing and painting if I had to find a way to support myself with it. But, thank you. Your opinion means a lot to me."

Even though Michael didn't want to relinquish the sketch pad, he set it down on the backseat where he'd found it. He didn't let the topic go as easily. "At the very least, your work should be on display somewhere."

Gavin laughed as he turned right from the parking lot into traffic. "Now you're just flattering me."

"That's not in my blood," Michael shot back without thought. The last thing Gavin needed was someone stroking his ego. Hell would freeze before Michael was the one doing it.

Gavin went quiet long enough to make Michael regret his words. When he finally spoke, it was slow, as if confessing a dirty secret. "I've thought several times about trying to get my work in galleries, or at least having a few prints in stores. If nothing else, I might frame some stuff for my house."

"You don't even have it framed in your house?" Even Michael heard the disbelief in his voice. He didn't know why it bugged him so much Gavin was still hiding that part of himself, but it did.

Gavin shrugged but kept his gaze locked on the road. "It's been hard enough for my parents to swallow the fact that I'm gay. I'm just trying not to rock the boat any more than necessary. One of these days, I'll get to be me. Maybe."

It was hard for Michael to picture Gavin's life. Michael's parents had always known he was gay and didn't care. He wanted to ask how things had gone when Gavin had finally come out, but he also felt the need to change the subject to happier times. Before he could think of a way to save their conversation, Gavin found a way to rescue them.

"What do you do in your spare time?"

Even though Gavin wasn't looking at him, Michael still shrugged. "I don't really have free time, per se. My life pretty much belongs to Mara, but I do have a lot of downtime while waiting to get her from point A to point B. Mostly, I just play games on my phone. I'm pretty boring these days." Michael thought about it for half a second before adding, "I guess I've always been boring. Why did you want to have lunch with me again?" he asked with a laugh.

"Hush," Gavin said. Laughter shone heavily in his voice. "I think you're amazing, always have."

Just not as amazing as Marshall. That thought was like a shot to the chest. It took all of Michael's willpower not to say it aloud. Instead, he focused on the road and tried his damnedest to keep the hurt from his voice. "Where are we headed?" There. Maybe he'd make it through this day after all.

———

Michael sounded so damn sad, and Gavin didn't understand what he'd done wrong. He was always on thin ice with Michael. "You'll see," Gavin said, inflicting as much playfulness as he could into his voice. He couldn't talk Michael around. The only way he'd win Michael was by proving himself. Today was the first step.

Michael shrugged and held his silence through the forty-five-minute drive. Even as they pulled into the parking lot of a park near the river, Michael didn't say a word. He glanced around, taking in the sights. It was a perfect day for this.

With the SUV in park, Gavin fished around

behind Michael's seat and grabbed a cooler. "We're having a picnic."

The way Michael's mouth lifted in one corner gave Gavin hope he'd made the right decision. Michael was like him—he loved the outdoors. Not only was this romantic, or so he'd been told, but it also gave them some privacy to talk. God knew they had a lot of shit they needed to say to each other.

"Where are we? This place seems familiar," Michael said as they climbed from the SUV and headed for a nearby table.

Gavin set the cooler on the picnic table and looked around. It had been years since he'd been there. "This is the first place we met."

A scoffing noise came from the back of Michael's throat. "No, it's not," he argued as he threw one leg over the bench and sat sideways, holding Gavin's stare. "The first place we met was gym class our Freshman year. You hit me with a volleyball because you were pissed off that you'd missed a shot when you jumped in front of me and knocked me out of the way."

Gavin shrugged. "Volleyball is a brutal sport. That's not the first place we met. I met you here." A chuckle rose in his throat as he finished his thoughts. "I hit you with a Frisbee."

As Gavin looked on, Michael's lips twisted into a

smile. He bit his bottom lip, trying to fight it. Gavin had never wanted to kiss anyone as badly in his life. Michael opened his mouth and killed the moment. "That wasn't me. That was Marshall."

"Liar," Gavin said, sounding accusing even to his ears. He couldn't help it. Marshall and Michael might get away with that shit with anyone else, but not him. Never him. "I was playing with Marshall. You were sitting in the grass, being weird, when I hit you with the Frisbee."

"I wasn't being weird," Michael said hotly, obviously forgetting his plan to lie. "I was plotting the destruction of my eighth grade teacher, Mr. Conner, for taking away my phone in class and keeping it all weekend. My parents were lawyers after all. I fully expected to have his job," Michael finished with a laugh.

"See? Being weird."

Michael laughed harder. "Maybe. Still, this moment makes me realize you had a pattern of hitting me with things."

Gavin moved as close as he could and opened the cooler. He did his best not to stare at Michael like a moonstruck fool. "I know they say not to tell kids that other kids hit them because they like them. In my case, that was true. I wanted your attention. Plus, as sexy as you are, you're a million times that when your eyes are flashing with outrage." Gavin chuckled and glanced over. "I wanted you to punish me." He handed Michael a sandwich and a bottle of water. "Here. I made everything myself, except the water... obviously." Damn, Gavin wanted to punch himself in the face. He sounded like such an idiot. It wasn't that he was uncomfortable. He didn't want to fuck this up. If he alienated Michael now, the dude might not ever give him another shot.

Michael unwrapped the sandwich and peeked between the slices of bread. "I completely believe you could create water," he said, taking a bite. "You're the most capable person I know," Michael added around his food.

Gavin concentrated on unwrapping his food, hoping Michael wouldn't see how moved he was by the man's words. They'd only been in each other's company for an hour, and already Michael had reminded him of all the reasons he couldn't stay away. How many other men in the world would see him the way Michael did? None, because Michael was the only one who Gavin would damn-well find a way to create water for if he needed it.

"I'm glad I agreed to this. This is nice," Michael said, surprising Gavin enough to turn his head. "Thank you," Michael added when he had Gavin's attention.

Gavin fought the urge to downplay his actions and lost. "It's no big deal. Anyone can make sandwiches."

"If you plan to keep spending time with me, you'll have to stop that." Michael kept his eyes locked on the food in his hands as he made the claim. He took another bite.

Gavin was fascinated by the way Michael's jaw moved while he chewed. It was sexy. "Stop what?"

"Making light of everything I compliment you on," Michael said, continuing to eat. "I compliment your art. You say it's a time killer. I thank you for lunch. You say it's no big deal."

For a moment, Gavin could only stare at Michael. He did all those things, but he had a good reason. "I don't want to sound like a conceited ass, and lunch really was no big deal. This is nothing compared to what I would do to spend time with you."

Michael's gaze slid his way. Gavin stopped breathing. It had been a damn long time since Michael looked at him with heat in his eyes. "Being a conceited ass always worked for you in the past. You should show me the rest of your paintings sometime."

"I have an out-of-town game tomorrow night. How about the night after that?"

Michael's gaze dropped to Gavin's mouth before

moving back to hold his stare. Gavin was hard enough to bend steel. "I'll take you to dinner first."

As much as Gavin didn't want Michael paying for anything, he wasn't missing his chance to spend more time with the man. "Sounds like a date." Goddamn, Gavin hoped it was, because he needed more of this —Michael's heated glances and compliments that swelled his head.

CHAPTER FOUR

*D*inner went better than Michael could've imagined and was over before he was ready. Food came and went. He must've eaten, but he barely remembered it. Gavin kept him mesmerized. He'd driven, so he could get the tour of Gavin's house after dinner and then leave. Michael didn't think Gavin was the type to keep him if he didn't want to stay, but Michael needed the illusion of control when it came to this man. As it was, Gavin touched him too much. Every time Michael turned around, the man set his hand on the small of Michael's back or cupped his elbow, steering him. He'd held Michael's hand in the restaurant and set his hand on Michael's leg in the car. There wasn't a single brush of skin Michael wasn't aware of as it happened.

As Gavin unlocked the front door to his two-story home and led Michael inside, Michael's heartrate increased and his stomach turned over. He couldn't remember the last time he'd been so nervous. Even though Michael knew he could leave at any time, he wasn't positive he wanted to. That was the scariest part.

"Would you like a bottle of water?"

Michael's dry throat made it hard to answer. "I'd love one. Thank you."

Gavin turned on the lights in the living room and motioned toward a brown leather couch. "I'll be back." He tossed his keys on the coffee table before exiting the room.

Michael sat. Everything was perfect. The hardwood floors shone bright. The oak tables were perfectly polished. There didn't seem to be a speck of dust anywhere. Trophies lined a bookcase while leather-bound books filled another. A large flat-screen hung over a stone fireplace. Michael didn't know what to do with his eyes. Giving in to his discomfort, he leaned to the side and dug his phone out of his back pocket.

MichaelThePA: *I built a static fusion fence around our camp.*

#1HatTrick: *Hey! What are you up to tonight?*

MichaelThePA: *On a date, of sorts.*

#1HatTrick: *It must not be that great of a date if you're building a fence.*

MichaelThePA: *I did it earlier. Things are going better than I expected, I suppose.*

#1HatTrick: *Question. Is this the guy you used to know?*

MichaelThePA: *Yes.*

#1HatTrick: *The plot thickens...*

Michael's fingers hovered over the buttons. He didn't know how to respond. Gavin reappeared with a cold bottle of water for Michael.

"Texting someone else already. Am I boring you?"

"Not at all," Michael said, setting the phone on the coffee table. "I was clearing out some notifications on an online game I play," he added as he accepted the bottle of water.

"That's good," Gavin said, setting one knee on the couch beside Michael and leaning in, as if to kiss him. "I thought maybe I needed to step up my game."

Michael turned his head without thought. A spike of fear raced through him at the thought of Gavin's lips on his. Instead, Gavin pressed a light kiss to the spot beneath Michael's ear. He didn't back away.

"What's the worst that could happen if you kissed me?"

Michael swallowed. He didn't want to answer. His

tongue didn't care. "I could remember what it was like."

Gavin's lips skimmed lower. He wasn't giving up. "You already remember me."

"No." Even Michael heard it for the lie it was.

With a sigh, Gavin straightened away. "So, I have to remind you," he said, taking away the water he'd just given Michael and setting it next to his phone. He pulled Michael to his feet.

"What are you doing?" Michael's panic couldn't have been more evident.

Gavin's low chuckle kept Michael focused on him. "I'm giving you a tour of my house and refreshing your memory of me." Michael's shoulders relaxed. A tour was fine as long as they avoided the bedroom. Gavin's house was gorgeous, but that wasn't surprising considering he lived in the same neighborhood they'd grown up in, two streets over from where Michael's parents still lived. Gavin held his hand as he headed for the hall. Michael wondered if he should drag his feet and bring this whole thing to an end. Gavin motioned at the kitchen, waving toward it as they passed. "The kitchen, obviously."

"Everyone needs one," Michael said with a nod. It was a nice kitchen too. Everything was granite and marble. Gorgeous. Not as gorgeous as Gavin, though, and that was why Michael couldn't stop staring at the man's back. He'd seen it without a shirt many times, but Gavin had changed a lot. How did his chest look now? Had his light smattering of hair turned into a bear's chest? Michael bit the inside of his cheek to keep from asking.

"The bathroom," Gavin said as they passed another open doorway.

This time, Michael didn't bother looking away. "Another great amenity every home needs."

"My bedroom is at the end of the hall." Michael's gaze slid that way. The room at the end of the hall was dark. Curiosity ate him alive, but Gavin turned left and headed for a set of stairs. Every house on this street was built on a hill. You entered in the house already on the second floor. Michael's curiosity doubled. Why did Gavin need so much space? "This is what you came to see," he said over his shoulder.

Michael's breath caught at the back of his throat at the glimmer in Gavin's eyes. "Is it?"

Gavin nodded and kept moving. At the bottom of the stairs, he flipped on a light switch and lit up a huge room. Michael's heart stopped before racing up again. It was an art studio. The whole place was like looking at the inside of Gavin's gorgeous mind. Michael couldn't stop trying to look in every direction at once.

"Wow," he breathed, moving toward a nearby

easel. A watercolor image half complete sat waiting for Gavin's return. Michael couldn't tell yet what it was meant to be, but he knew Gavin had a vision for it. He moved to a table where several smaller canvases sat drying. Michael eyed each one. He froze when he came to an image of himself. "It's me."

Gavin moved in behind him. His chest brushed Michael's back as he leaned over Michael's shoulder. "You're beautiful. I've always loved painting you."

"The detail is amazing," Michael said, ignoring Gavin's compliment. "I can't believe you did this from memory."

"I don't forget much," Gavin said, his mouth closer to the back of Michael's neck than Michael expected. He fingered the back of Michael's collar. "Like the freckle on your nape." He tugged Michael's shirt aside and touched his lips to the spot he described. "I've kissed it a hundred times," Gavin said against Michael's skin.

Michael couldn't breathe. He white-knuckled the edge of the table, clinging to control. His cock beat a pattern against the inside of his zipper. A tiny voice in his head screamed for him to shove Gavin away. He couldn't move. Gavin's lips moved over Michael's freckle again. His hands landed on Michael's upper arms and squeezed. He tugged, drawing Michael back against his hard body. The man's lips moved from

Michael's nape to his shoulder. A pant escaped Michael. He wanted this, but he couldn't let it happen. Gavin would wreck him. Michael had survived him once. He wasn't as sure he could do it twice.

"I should go," Michael said, sounding weak even to his ears.

"Okay," Gavin said, stepping back. He sounded disappointed. He may as well have punched Michael. Michael lost his breath and nearly gasped from the pain in his chest.

He scrambled to fix it. Michael turned and wrapped his arms around Gavin, hugging him. He held tight. Gavin's arms encircled him. They held each other. Michael didn't know how long it went on. He didn't want their embrace to end. "Thank you for going to dinner with me," Michael said quietly.

"I enjoyed myself," Gavin said. His hold tightened as if he didn't want to let Michael go.

Michael flattened his palms against Gavin's back. The man's hard muscles bunched and rolled beneath Michael's hands, as if he fought not to attack Michael.

"Spend tomorrow with me," Michael said before he could think about it. He wasn't ready to give up yet.

"Okay."

At Gavin's agreement, Michael gave the man one final squeeze before heading for the stairs without looking back. He was scared of himself. If he looked, he might stay, and then this would be over.

———

Gavin watched Michael go. It killed him not to call out, stopping him. He had to plant his feet to keep from giving chase. Michael wanted to see him tomorrow. It would have to be enough. The instant Michael was out of sight, Gavin moved to the easel. That freckle drove him. Gavin had an image in his mind. He could see each time he'd kissed that spot as if he did so now in front of a mirror. Gavin needed to move the energy of the moment from his mind and onto the canvas board before it made him insane.

As Gavin painted, images of Michael swirled in his head. He'd waited a long time to come back to Michael. The last thing Gavin had wanted was to make the same mistakes. He'd needed to grow up and make sure he could handle this open life before going after the only man he wanted. Now, it was harder to be patient than he expected.

He could still hear their every whispered conversation and picture every heated glance. His chest ached and his body screamed. Gavin scared even himself with this obsession. If Michael was a little freaked out, and that was why he'd run away tonight, Gavin couldn't blame him. Michael had moved on—lived another life. He should be scared of Gavin because Gavin hadn't moved on. One hundred percent, he knew he was crazy. That Michael was a sickness. At the end of the day, his mental stability didn't matter. No one would love Michael the way Gavin did.

Gavin's phone buzzed. He set his brush aside and dug the device from his pocket.

Michael: *What are you doing right now?*

Gavin: *Painting.*

Michael: *Get back to it then.*

A smile tugged at the corners of Gavin's mouth. He had to take a breath to control his heartbeat. Had Michael even made it home yet? Gavin checked his watch. He blinked at the time. Two hours had passed while he'd withdrawn into himself.

Gavin: *I will, but first tell me what you're doing.*

Gavin chewed his bottom lip and stared at his phone, anticipating. Thankfully, Michael didn't make him wait long.

Michael: *I'm in bed, but I can't sleep. In truth, I don't sleep much anymore.*

Without moving his gaze from his phone, Gavin headed for a recliner in the corner. It was old and ragged, but broken in perfectly. Gavin crashed there most nights when he lost track of time while painting. He kicked back and fired off another text.

Gavin: *There's an old chair down here. Usually, I paint until I'm exhausted, and then fall into it half asleep. Why don't you sleep?*

Michael: *My mind is busy, I guess.*

Gavin: *What's on your mind tonight?*

He held his breath and waited, needing to know what thoughts kept Michael's mind stirring.

Michael: *You. Us. I don't know. I keep remembering things, and then I can't forget. Then I start obsessing.*

Gavin: *What did you remember tonight?*

Michael: *That weekend Marshall went to Arkansas to tour a college.*

The muscles in Gavin's stomach contracted. Lust coiled in his gut. They'd been alone for an entire weekend. It had been forty-eight hours out of time— a suspension of reality. Gavin had caught a glimpse of a different life. They hadn't made love. That was one line Michael never let him cross as if he'd known Gavin wasn't man enough yet. But they'd done everything else, and Gavin hadn't stopped smiling for two weeks afterward. His hand slid to his groin. He readjusted his hardening cock.

Gavin: *That was a good weekend, and an exhausting one. The memory should put you to sleep.*

Michael: *Get back to painting. I have to think about what I want to do tomorrow.*

Gavin: *Yes, sir. Goodnight.*

Michael: *Goodnight.*

Gavin stared at the face of his phone until it went black. Even then, he didn't look away. His mind was in bed with Michael, debating how they should spend their time. One day soon, his fantasies would be real. There was no other option for him.

———

With his phone resting against his chest, Michael stared at the darkened ceiling. After texting Gavin, that weekend they'd spent alone years ago seemed even clearer in his mind than before. It was that weekend that hurt the most once they were over. He'd been certain they were only months away from living that way always, the moment they were free of school and gossipy teens. They hadn't held on long enough.

Still, that weekend lived in his head. The way Gavin's mouth felt on his skin when Michael was on the edge of orgasm. Damn. It had been so goddamn long since anyone touched him. He could still feel Gavin's body against him from when they'd hugged earlier. Gavin's muscles were fucking amazing. The way they'd pressed against each other — sternum to hip — Michael craved so much more. He wished he'd been brave enough to reach for more. Michael's hand dipped beneath the covers. He readjusted his slowly hardening cock. His warm palm felt too good against his erection once it was there. Michael closed his eyes and rubbed his cock through his underwear. It wasn't enough. He set his erection free.

His lips parted on a breath when his fingers encircled his dick. Still, a slight dissatisfaction filled him. It wasn't Gavin. Gavin's almost-amber gaze wasn't watching his every reaction, ensuring his every move brought Michael the most pleasure. It was too late to stop. Michael pushed the covers down until cool air brushed his exposed cock. He stroked himself while picturing it was Gavin touching him. Adding a second hand to the mix, Michael cupped his balls and squeezed as he jacked off. Fantasies of lowering himself on Gavin's hard dick fired to life behind Michael's closed lids. Michael felt so fucking empty. He was tempted to jump from the bed and grab a toy, but he was too far gone. Pressure already beat at his crown, begging for release. The memory of Gavin's expression when he came slammed into Michael's mind. An orgasm hit Michael hard. All the air left his lungs as Gavin's name left his lips. Wave after wave of cum coated his skin. He squeezed out every drop.

Michael didn't move once it was over. Even as the air cooled the mess covering him, he didn't budge an inch. His mind went into lockdown. Pain filled every inch of Michael, crippling him. A tear slipped from the corner of his eye, falling back into Michael's hair. It was too late. The invisible weight crushing the air from his lungs told the whole story. The clock was already ticking down. He didn't have to worry about Gavin getting under his skin. The man had never left, and it was only a matter of time before Gavin destroyed him, because Michael wouldn't wake up tomorrow and be the person Gavin wanted. He wouldn't wake up tomorrow and be Marshall.

CHAPTER FIVE

*G*avin: *There are club-level tickets for you at the will-call booth in Shreveport for my next game on Saturday. See you there.*

Michael: *Um. What?*

Gavin: *You said you like it when I'm conceited and controlling. I'm being both. Saturday night. Shreveport Arena. 7pm. I'll see you there.*

Michael: *Yeah, I'm pretty sure I didn't say that. I'll have to check my schedule, and that's a five-hour drive.*

Gavin: *Shreveport.*

Michael: *Fine, but I'm driving back home afterward.*

Gavin: *We'll see.*

Michael: *I suppose we will.*

———

It wasn't like Michael to feel out of place. He was used to being alone. That was why he had such a hard time understanding why he felt like everyone was looking at him. He'd tried walking around. It wasn't the first time he'd been club level for a game. Normally, at hockey games, he was with Mara and was always in high style. There was no reason for his feeling of unease, but Michael couldn't sit still. A hand landed on his shoulder, nearly making Michael jump out of his skin, and that was before he turned to set eyes on the most beautiful man on the planet. In fact, he really was. Ryker De Blanc was one of the hottest underwear models in the world. There wasn't a man or woman alive who hadn't seen the man's sexy body in all its glory.

"We were wondering if you'd like to join us," Ryker said with a sexy English accent and drawing attention to the fact that he wasn't alone. A brown-haired, blue-eyed dude stood at his side. Two other men stood at their backs. Ryker motioned toward the man beside him. "This is my husband Grady."

Grady held out his hand for Michael to shake. "Nice to meet you."

Michael accepted. "You too." Even Michael heard the question in his voice. They all acted as if they knew him, but he'd yet to introduce himself.

Ryker motioned at the men behind him. "This is

Lincoln and Shayne. We're friends of Gavin's," he clarified.

The man named Shayne stepped forward. "Gavin texted me before the game and let me know you'd be here. He didn't want you sitting alone."

"Oh," Michael said for lack of anything else. "I'm used to being alone," Michael added, horrifying even himself. He had no idea why he'd admitted to such a thing.

"Nonetheless," Ryker said, wearing a sweet smile, "we're having dinner over there," he said, motioning toward a nearby table where a well-dressed man sat alone. "You should join us."

Since Michael couldn't look away from Ryker's mismatched eyes, he agreed. At least this way, he could stare at Ryker without being too obvious about it. "If you're okay with me joining you, I'd love to." Michael shifted his gaze Grady's way as he made the claim. He'd learned a long time ago to ensure his gaze said he wasn't interested in anything other than friendship. Spouses of celebrities could be a jealous and volatile lot. Grady's smile seemed nice. Michael kept his head down and made his way toward to the table. When he reached the edge, the only man left sitting stood.

He pulled the chair beside him out for Michael to sit. "You've chosen to join us. Lovely," the man said with a heavy Russian accent. "I am Maksim Petrov, and you are the sexy Michael Frost."

Michael smiled. He didn't bother asking how everyone knew him. They'd obviously been discussing him before deciding as a group to invite him over. "It's nice to meet you," Michael said, accepting the man's offer to sit.

"I hear you work for Mara King," Grady said as soon as Michael was settled.

He had a hard time picturing Gavin telling such a thing and was more than a little bothered by it for some reason. Still, he couldn't deny it. "Yes. I'm her PA and handler."

Maksim nodded. "See?" he said to the table at large. "I do not lie. I heard it from the Kieran Steele himself." Ah. That explained a lot. Fuck. Everyone knew Kieran, and that man wasn't above dropping a name.

Shayne nodded. "I love her movies. You must have an amazing life."

Michael nodded. "She's great. What do the rest of you do? Obviously, not you," Michael said to Ryker. "I've seen your face on every magazine." Damn, he had to stop himself from blushing as he said the words. Luckily, Ryker nodded, as if he hadn't expected less. It was odd. There didn't seem to be an ounce of conceit to Ryker. He was a bit quiet and reserved. The man also kept sneaking glances at his husband as if he thought the man hung the moon. A spike of jealousy ran through Michael. He wished someone would look at him like that.

Shayne spoke up, saving Michael from his bleak thoughts. "I'm in charge of media relations for the Blue Fires. That's how I know Gavin." He linked fingers with the man sitting beside him. "This is my husband, Lincoln. He's a doctor." Shayne sounded so proud, Michael couldn't stop his smile.

Grady chimed in, "I'm a retired cop. Nowadays, I spend all my time traveling with Ryker. He needs someone watching his back, you know?"

"I'm sure," Michael said before he could stop himself. Grady laughed, smoothing over the awkward moment.

Maksim touched his arm, dragging Michael's attention his way. "I am one of those no-good talent scouts who stalks these games, looking to scoop up all the good players. But I give them money, so s'okay."

"Can I buy you something to eat?" Ryker said, as if intentionally keeping Michael's attention off Maksim. Michael understood. It was obvious the too-slick Russian was a player. Michael recognized all the signs. Ryker need not worry. Michael only had eyes for Gavin.

"I'm fine," Michael said, already feeling like he was interrupting their dinner.

"Let me rephrase that," Ryker said, smiling. "I'm buying you dinner. What would you like? They actually have healthy options here. No poisonous grease like you find in fast food places."

Michael blinked. "No poison is always a good thing."

The crowd roared, pulling everyone's attention toward the ice. "Gavin Weeks has pulled off another perfect hat trick. The forward is the number one leader of hat tricks in the league and is in line to beat the record held since 1952."

"Your man is quite the catch," Maksim said. "I've been eyeing him for some time."

Michael searched for a double meaning in Maksim's words but heard none. "Any team would be lucky to have him," Michael said out of loyalty.

Maksim's dark blue eyes shone heavy with some unnamed emotion. Michael was afraid to look too deeply. "Seems to me he is very lucky to have you."

Michael blinked at the compliment. He didn't know how to react.

Maksim didn't let him stew for long. "As it happens, New York has been after Gavin for a while."

"I'm sure he'll go for the right offer." Michael wondered if he should take up acting. He wanted

Gavin to be happy. It was like a knife to the heart, thinking about Gavin moving away. Michael's phone chirped, alerting him of an incoming message. He hated to be rude, but he was also always on call. Michael tried checking his phone beneath the table. It was Mara, so he couldn't ignore it.

Mara: *Are you still in Shreveport?*

Michael: *Yes. Do you need me to come back?*

Mara: *No. I need you to stay there. Have you seen the weather?*

Michael: *No. I've been busy watching the game. What did I miss?*

Mara: *That flash flood has turned into a monsoon. The road to your house is flooded. I talked to your neighbor, and she said your house is fine, but no one can get in or out of your neighborhood. I would feel better if you would just stay there for the night. A lot of the roads around town are getting bad. I'll send you a link to the flood map, so you can see for yourself.*

Michael checked the link. Fuck. It looked like he would be better off in Shreveport. Several main roads were at or above flood stage. Before he realized what he was doing, Michael found himself searching the roads surrounding Gavin's house as well. Damn, it looked like he couldn't get home either. Not that it mattered. He'd traveled there with his team and already had a room.

Michael: *Thanks for letting me know. I'll be back as soon as the roads are passable.*

Mara: *Don't worry over me. Just take care of yourself. I'll see you when it's safe.*

"Anyone know any good hotels?" Michael asked the table at large. "Looks like the roads are washing out back home."

A round of groans went up around the table, letting him know he wasn't the only one who'd intended to go home after this. He felt his first click of common ground with the men. Michael hoped they'd all meet again someday.

———

Michael appeared in the mouth of the dressing room, looking sexy as sin and unsure of his welcome. Gavin had never been prouder to have someone waiting for him. It had been the world's longest game, waiting to get to Michael. He tossed his towel aside, heading in Michael's direction with tunnel vision. The rest of the world disappeared.

"Hey." Even to Gavin's ears, he sounded breathless.

Michael's mouth lifted in one corner. His green eyes, which lived in Gavin's mind, shone bright with interest. "Hey."

Goddamn it. Gavin wished Michael would let him kiss him. It was beyond frustrating trying to overcome the past. "How much time do I have with you before you head back to New Orleans?"

His shoulders lifted. "Looks like you have all night," Michael said, taking him by surprise. "Mara texted me earlier, saying the road to my house has been temporarily washed out by the flash flood. So it seems I need to find a room here."

"Or you could stay in mine," Gavin offered, even though he knew Michael wouldn't accept.

"Or I could stay in yours," Michael agreed, taking Gavin by surprise.

It took every ounce of Gavin's self-control not to take off running for the car right then. He also fought to keep his face clear of all triumph. "It's still early. Are you hungry?" Damn, he deserved a medal for keeping his excitement from his voice.

"Some guy named Ryker fed me, but I'm fine to go wherever if you're hungry."

Fuck. Ryker? He was married, but still. No one could compete with Ryker's beauty. The dude was literally the hottest male model in the world. He'd fed Michael? Gavin had so many questions. "Ryker was here tonight? His husband must've been here with Shayne." There. He'd managed to throw Ryker's husband, Grady, into the mix and everything.

Michael nodded. "I met Shayne, Lincoln, and Grady. Oh, and some guy named Maksim. They all seemed like nice people."

Fuck him twice. He'd met Maksim too. That was it. He could never invite Michael to another game alone. Maksim was single and ruthless. No doubt he already had Michael's name programmed in his phone, and Michael didn't know how it happened. That was how Maksim worked.

"So, are you hungry?" Michael asked, looking uncomfortable and making Gavin realize how long he'd been standing there lost in thought.

Gavin nodded. "A little. We could find a store so you can buy anything you need for an overnight trip, and I could just grab something there since you've eaten already."

"That works for me. Do you need to tell anyone you're out?"

"Nope, I'm good," Gavin said, reaching for Michael's hand and heading for the back door. "Do you remember where you parked?"

Michael glanced down at their joined hands, but didn't try pulling away. "Not really, but I'm sure we'll find it."

As the back door came into view, their steps slowed. The bottom was falling out of the sky. Rain came down in sheets. They exchanged smiles. "We're about to get soaked, looking for your car."

"Yep," Michael said, sounding entirely too happy about it.

He'd forgotten. Michael loved the rain. More times than he could count, he'd seen Michael stand outside during a storm, smiling as his clothes molded to his skin. Gavin was almost glad Michael couldn't remember where he'd parked. He intentionally walked slow, under the guise of searching for Michael's car. Gavin spotted it under a nearby light. He nodded in its direction. "There. Hey, do you want to skip the store until we can get dry or I can lend you some stuff?"

Michael glanced over and smiled. "That's probably for the best. Of course, anything you lend me will probably swallow me whole."

"But, damn, you'd look sexy with my clothes hanging off your gorgeous body." Gavin couldn't even find it in his heart to regret the words. He could already picture Michael wearing his clothes.

Instead of responding, Michael headed for the car without a word. The lights flashed when they got close. Gavin went over everything he'd said, wondering if he'd gone too far. Damn, he was tired of second guessing himself all the time. All Gavin wanted

was to be with Michael. Happy. Gavin gave directions
to his hotel room while still trying to decide his next
move. Obviously, if Michael wouldn't even kiss him,
he wouldn't be in Gavin's bed tonight, but he'd have
Michael to himself for the whole night. Surely he
could make some progress. The hotel came into sight.
Between the rain and the bad lighting, he could barely
see a thing. Luckily, Michael got a parking space near
the door. Before he could kill the car, one of Gavin's
favorite songs came on. It was an old love song that
never got old in Gavin's book. It said everything he
felt about waiting for the one to come back.

Without thought, he grabbed Michael's arm,
stopping him from turning off the song. "I have an
idea. Don't move," Gavin said, leaping from the car
and circling around to Michael's side. He opened the
door and held his hand out to Michael. "Turn it up
and dance with me."

Michael's smile made the ridiculous offer
worthwhile. "Here?"

Gavin nodded. "Right here. In the rain."

He half expected Michael to swat his hand away.
Instead, his smile grew as he turned the song up and
let Gavin pull him from the car. "I always let you talk
me into shit," Michael said as his body molded
against Gavin's. Gavin could barely hear a word past
the blood rushing through his ears. Michael had let

him hug him, and he'd stolen a few touches and kisses on Michael's neck. This was the closest Michael had let him get since they'd started seeing each other again. It still wasn't close enough. Gavin touched his lips to the side of Michael's neck, ignoring Michael's claim. He quietly sang against the man's skin, hoping he would understand every word was for him. They barely moved. In truth, it was more of a long hug than a dance. Gavin didn't care. He felt every second in his chest. Michael's arms tightened around him. His fingers found the edge of Gavin's shirt and dove beneath, stroking Gavin's back skin on skin. Rain beat down on them. Gavin's heart soaked up every second.

"Gavin?"

Gavin's heart turned over at the sound of Michael whispering his name. "Yeah?"

"People are looking out their window at us."

A chuckle escaped Gavin. He didn't care if people stared at them all night, but he'd hate for them to call management or the police, thinking they were drunk. That would dampen their night. He sighed. "I guess we should go inside before we're answering to the cops, and we're probably ruining the interior of your car."

He felt Michael hesitate as he pulled away. Gavin wanted to beg for the man's thoughts. Michael leaned inside the car and killed the ignition before closing the door. "It's Mara's car, so I guess I shouldn't ruin it."

"Yeah," Gavin said past his rapidly tightening throat. He got the feeling he'd missed his chance to tell Michael how much he loved him... again.

———

Michael stared at Gavin's back as he unlocked the hotel room door. His clothes were plastered to his skin, showing off every deep line of muscle. It was hot, but Michael's ever-growing obsession had nothing do with Gavin's looks. He'd forgotten how amazing Gavin could be when he wasn't being a dick. Every second he spent in Gavin's presence made him crave ten seconds more. He'd never been more frightened of depending on someone in his life, but Michael knew it wouldn't be much longer before being with Gavin was all he wanted to do.

"Holy shit. It's like I showered in my clothes," Gavin said, laughing as he closed the door behind them. Michael couldn't look away. Gavin looked so damn happy as he reached over his head and tried peeling his shirt off. He'd been right. Gavin's smattering of light hair had turned into a bear's chest. Michael's resistance fell. He couldn't take another second without touching Gavin. While Gavin's shirt still covered his eyes, Michael closed the distance between them and captured the man's mouth. His skin was like ice beneath Michael's hands. Gavin went still, making Michael feel like he was kissing a statue. He immediately backed away. It had been a ridiculous sentiment. Gavin yanked his shirt the rest of the way off and tossed it aside. Heat blazed in the man's gaze when he focused on Michael. Michael fought the urge to take another step back. There was nowhere to go.

"Don't do something you don't mean," Gavin warned.

Michael's throat wouldn't work. Not that it mattered. He didn't know what to say. Instead of speaking, he stared at Gavin—helpless. There wasn't a doubt in his mind that his every emotion was written all over his face. The only time in his life when he'd felt alive was when he was with Gavin. He wanted everything. Fuck it. He'd let Gavin take charge the last time they'd been together. Not this time. Without another thought, he closed the distance between them once more and captured Gavin's mouth. He'd missed the way Gavin nipped at his lips and sucked on his tongue. Too many times to count, he'd slid his hand beneath the covers and stroked himself to the memory. No matter how many times he touched himself with Gavin's name on his lips, he couldn't recreate the sensation of Gavin touching him.

"You look so fucking sexy, wearing my name across your back," Gavin said, fingering the jersey Michael wore that had Gavin's name stitched across the back. "I hate to take this off, but I need your bare skin," Gavin said, working the wet shirt over Michael's head before coming back for more.

Michael didn't play. He didn't pretend he wasn't after everything. His hands went for Gavin's belt, sliding the leather loose. "I've missed everything about you," Michael admitted with stinging eyes and no shame. Two months ago, he would've eaten shit before saying those words, but now he couldn't hold them back. Between kisses and bites, confessions continued pouring out. "You're my biggest regret."

"Don't say that," Gavin begged, sounding desperate.

Michael shushed him. "It's not for what you think. I regretted all the times I told you no. You've lived in the back of mind, torturing me with wondering how we'd fit. If we'd be as perfect as I expected. I need to know."

To his surprise, Gavin stepped around him, leaving Michael staring at the man's sexy back as he walked away. Hurt crippled him. He'd exposed his heart to Gavin. Gavin walked to the edge of the bed and turned down the covers. Michael watched it happen while still trying to grasp what was happening.

Gavin slipped his belt loose from the loops of his jeans and tossed it aside before digging out his loose change and tossing it on the side table. Still, Michael could only watch. Gavin pulled his wallet from his back pocket before finally meeting Michael's gaze.

His eyebrows were raised in question as if he didn't understand why Michael hadn't moved. "Why aren't you undressed and in bed yet?" Gavin said the words so calmly Michael didn't react right away. He didn't know what he'd been expecting. Maybe he'd thought his confession would have Gavin tossing him over his shoulder like a caveman. This was better— like Gavin felt the way Michael did—a calm acceptance they were meant to be together.

Michael's feet finally unglued from the floor. He toed off his shoes and unbuttoned his pants as he headed for the bed. There was no discomfort. They'd been here before. Not to mention, the way Gavin eyed him, as if he was the sexiest man on the planet, drove Michael out of his clothes faster than he thought possible. On his back and waiting, Michael watched Gavin dig a condom from his wallet before shedding the rest of his clothes. The man's body was perfect. He'd always been. Michael hadn't forgotten, but Gavin was larger now—more muscular. Gavin's gorgeous gaze never wavered from Michael. Michael's dick throbbed and ached. Each breath he took came harder than the last. He needed everything Gavin's eyes promised.

"This condom is lubricated, but it's all I have with me," Gavin said as he set one knee on the mattress and rolled the condom over his length.

Michael gave him a short nod, letting him know he understood. His throat wouldn't work.

"I don't want to hurt you," Gavin said, clarifying as if Michael's nod hadn't been enough.

"My chest hurts waiting for you to decide if you want me." Michael had no idea why he'd said such a thing. He couldn't take the pressure of Gavin moving so slow.

A small smile touched Gavin's lips, making Michael's mouth go dry. "Not a day has gone by that I haven't thought of you and wanted you," Gavin said as he settled between Michael's thighs. "I'm trying to give you one last chance to back down. You'll always be mine, even if you never are, but after this, I won't let you walk away again."

"You've always talked too much," Michael said, pulling Gavin's mouth down to his. He was past hearing speeches or being given chances. It was time for Gavin to give him everything he'd stolen.

Gavin's tongue toyed with his. Michael's cock leaked on his stomach. Lust curled in his gut. There was a sexy man between his thighs and Michael wanted to feel him pressing his way inside. Unfortunately, Gavin didn't seem to be in the same hurry. Michael moved against him, silently seeking relief. His body felt empty without Gavin's cock filling him. Gavin's fingertips skimmed Michael's hip, so close to where Michael wanted to be touched. Frustration grew out of control. Michael cupped his balls and massaged, making the aggravation worse. Michael's heels dug into the mattress. He lifted his hips, shamelessly attempting to lure Gavin inside. Instead, Gavin's fingertip lightly traced the line between Michael's balls and asshole. Gavin's lips moved to Michael's jaw.

Michael broke as Gavin's fingertip circled his asshole. "Jesus, you're a tease. I thought you wanted —" Gavin pushed one finger inside, curling upward, hitting all the right places, and stealing Michael's voice. A low moan ripped from the back of his throat.

"Oh, shit, Mikey. You don't know how much I've missed hearing you make that sound." A much larger pressure pushed against the ring of muscles surrounding his asshole. Michael held his breath. "I wanted to go slow, but I need to hear you make that sound again," Gavin said, forcing his way inside an inch. Michael couldn't take it. He reached between their bodies and stroked himself. His dick needed attention. The temptation was too thick. Another moan filled the air. He was too far gone to know if he'd been the one to make the sound. Gavin's dick stretched him wide, filling him past completion as Gavin pushed inside another inch. Michael held Gavin's stare as Gavin finally completely impaled him. Gavin looked turned on and sexy.

"You're so fucking beautiful," Michael whispered without his brain's permission. He couldn't help it. If he ever stopped and took a moment to be honest with himself, Gavin had ruined him for all others a long time ago. He'd never looked at another soul and found them as Gavin's equal. It didn't matter this man had once broken his heart. Michael didn't want anyone else.

"You've always been it for me," Gavin said, mirroring Michael's thoughts so closely, he wondered for a moment if he'd spoken aloud. Michael lifted his head and kissed him. He needed to feel those words on Gavin's tongue. Gavin rocked against him, slow and torturing. He reached between them and pushed Michael's hand aside, claiming Michael's erection for himself. Michael nearly came right then. There it was. The way Gavin touched him. The way Michael had never been able to recreate. It was the strength and surety of his hands. The way his fingers moved. Michael was helpless. His hips lifted, mindlessly seeking more even as his tongue tried mimicking their bodies. Gavin fucked with his head. The way he made love made Michael feel loved. His heart couldn't detach. That love he hadn't been able to shake, even through years apart and no hope of reconnecting, fired to life as if a single day had barely passed. Michael couldn't breathe around the emotions choking him. His body was on fire and on edge while his mind was a mess.

Gavin tore his mouth away and sucked on Michael's shoulder. Pants and moans filled the room. "Fuck, baby," Gavin groaned. "I need you to come for me. I've wanted this too long. Not gonna last," he added, sounding ragged.

The idea of pushing Gavin past desperation, turning him on like this, had the pressure building in Michael's balls. He tried breathing through the tightening of his body. It was no use. Gavin had no mercy. He tugged Michael's cock until the pressure was too much. An explosion of light and ecstasy shook him from the inside. Liquid heat melded their bodies together as Michael rode out the waves.

Gavin gasped. "Holy shit, Mikey. Fuck.

Goddamn." The curses continued as Gavin pumped the condom full.

Michael couldn't look away from Gavin's pleasure-filled expression. Every muscle in the man's face had hardened as he orgasmed before going soft. Now his kiss-swollen lips and flushed cheeks completed the image. Michael knew he'd never forget. The sight was already seared into his brain. If they never touched again, he finally had his biggest dream come true. Gavin had looked at him as if he loved him too.

———

Holding Michael was heaven. It was everything he'd dreamed it would be. Michael kept stroking his arms and Gavin fought to stay awake. As the exhaustion and peace settled over him, Gavin's mind drifted. Memories rolled in.

The itch beneath his skin was especially bad tonight. Coach had a girl he wanted Gavin to meet. Apparently, she was some famous football player's niece who'd just moved to town. She didn't know anyone. It seemed his dad didn't know anyone either because he'd chosen Gavin to take her out this weekend. There was a sickness in the pit of his stomach. What if this was finally the time Michael broke? One of these days, it would happen. No one in their right mind would put up with as much as Michael did. When

Michael finally decided he was done with Gavin, it would kill him. What would happen to him when no one saw him any longer? Would he disappear?

He stubbed his toe as he headed to Michael's bed in the dark. Even though he could barely see, he saw Michael jump, as if Gavin had woken him.

"Sorry," Gavin whispered into the darkness.

Michael moved over, making room for him in the bed. Gavin didn't waste any time climbing beneath the covers and snuggling close. He could tell by the Michael's deep breathing that he was more asleep than awake. That was fine. Gavin just needed to hold him. Smell his skin. As his nose touched the side of Michael's neck and his familiar scent filled Gavin's nostrils, the backs of Gavin's eyes stung. It hurt more than he could voice, knowing he wouldn't get to keep the only person who mattered. Gavin hated himself more in that moment than he ever had. He hated his life. When Michael dumped him, maybe he'd drive his truck off a cliff. He didn't want to be invisible anymore.

Gavin buried his nose against Michael's throat and inhaled, as he'd done that night. Funny how not much had changed. Michael was still the only person who saw him or cared. Things were different now. He could and would be the person Michael deserved.

"You smell like this dream I had once," Gavin said. He felt Michael's lips shape a smile against his shoulder.

"Was it a good dream?"

Gavin inhaled again, trying to memorize every detail. "The best fucking dream in the world," Gavin admitted as sleep tried pulling him under. "You were there," Gavin confessed before moving even closer to Michael and letting the world fall away.

———

Michael couldn't sleep. He equally couldn't spend the entire night staring at Gavin like a lovesick puppy while Gavin slept. *You were there*. Those words kept floating through Michael's mind. It was taking every ounce of his restraint not to wake Gavin and steal another moment of his time. He'd stared at Gavin like this while he slept more times than he could count. It used to be so he could keep him safe...

A loud bang startled Michael from his dreams. He automatically moved over, making room for Gavin. The moment Gavin gathered him into his arms, Michael's heart ached. Gavin was having one of his nights—one of his bad moments. Michael could practically feel the hurt rolling off him in waves. This was why he let this sneaking around go on. He knew in his heart, if Gavin had any other choice, he'd treat Michael like a king. It was in the way he held Michael sometimes—like his life was ending because he knew they were only temporary. And Michael didn't doubt for a moment they were temporary. That never stopped Michael from dreaming.

After rolling to his side, Michael held Gavin closer and massaged every place he could reach, trying to ease his inner pain. He couldn't change things, but he could hold Gavin and give him hope. "What if we ran away?"

"Where would two teenagers go?" Gavin asked, sounding defeated.

"Not now," Michael clarified. "In a few months, we'll both be eighteen. Less than a month after that, we'll graduate. Let's pick a college a thousand miles from here. We could get a small apartment."

"I could paint while you study to get your law degree," Gavin said, adding to the fantasy.

"Once I have it, I'd make enough to support us while you open your own studio," Michael said, smiling against Gavin's chest.

Gavin kissed his forehead. His lips lingered against Michael's skin. "You make everything better."

Moments like these made everything bearable. Being held by Gavin made everything worthwhile.

That was still true. With a sigh, Michael leaned over the edge of the bed and dug through his clothes until he found his phone. Unfortunately, not sleeping was a familiar state for Michael. Luckily, he had a bullshit game to focus on instead.

MichaelThePA: *I see you cleared out the last of the enemies around the camp.*

Gavin's phone lit up on the bedside table, catching Michael's eye. He tried ignoring it. It wasn't any of his business who was calling in the middle of the night. At least, that was what he told himself. Otherwise, he might have to wake Gavin and kill him.

He checked on his game again. No response from #1HatTrick. Michael checked the time. It was one in the morning. No wonder the dude wasn't answering. Michael was the crazy one in this equation. Still, he messaged him again.

MichaelThePA: *Sorry. I guess you're sleeping.*

Gavin's phone lit again. Michael's gaze slid between their phones. That was odd. Michael did it again.

MichaelThePA: *I didn't realize how late it is.*

Sure enough, Gavin's phone lit again. That was too much to be a coincidence. Something niggled at the back of his mind. Michael clicked on #1HatTrick's avi picture. On his phone, it was too small to see it clearly without clicking on it and making it bigger. It just looked like a glob of colors. When the picture expanded, Michael's breath caught. He'd known when he'd gone through Gavin's sketchbook that the picture of the warrior elf looked familiar. It was the same avi he was looking at now. Everything clicked. Gavin held the number one spot in hat tricks in the league, nearing breaking the record. He couldn't fucking believe it. Without thought, he punched Gavin in the arm.

"Oh my fucking God. You're #1HatTrick."

Gavin jumped a foot, gasping as if ripped from a deep sleep. "What the fuck?"

Michael didn't back down. "That's my question. What the actual fuck? You're #1HatTrick."

"Oh," Gavin said, settling back down. He snagged Michael around the waist and tucked him underneath his large body, ensuring Michael couldn't get away.

"Don't 'oh' me and then settle down to cuddle like nothing happened. We've been messaging through this game for almost a year now."

Gavin held him tighter, making it harder and harder for Michael to be upset. "Settle down, baby. I'll tell you the story."

In spite of himself, Michael found himself snuggling even closer. "Okay." Gah. He hated how calm he sounded.

"A year or so ago, I was standing in Otto's coffee house."

"Hey, I go there all the time," Michael said, interrupting.

Gavin squeezed him and he fell silent. "Anyhow,"

Gavin said, trying to take back the conversation. "I was staring at the sign, trying to decide what I would get, even though I always get the same thing and, I swear, I smelled you. No matter how much time we've been apart, you've been in my head, and I knew it was you before I dropped my gaze and spotted that sexy freckle on the back of your neck. I couldn't believe it. You had your head bowed, staring down at your phone. There were literally only inches between our bodies. It was like nothing had changed. I had to fight the urge to drop my lips to your neck and kiss that freckle, the way I always do."

"Awww," Michael said, hating himself for being moved so easily.

"Obviously, I couldn't do that," Gavin said, staying on topic despite Michael's interruption. "But I was overwhelmed by how much I still wanted you in just one glance. So I watched you. You were playing some game on your phone, and you never noticed me. After you left, I couldn't shake it. While still sitting there at a table in the coffee shop, I pulled out my phone, downloaded the game, and searched the username I'd seen on your phone. It took me two weeks of nonstop playing to get myself in a position to approach you. I didn't really have a plan," Gavin said, sounding as if he was lost in thought. "All I knew was—it was a connection to you. I held on to it and waited."

Michael tensed. "Why do I get the feeling there's more?"

"Because you know I'm insane for you," Gavin said with a laugh.

"Oh," Michael said lamely. He wasn't sure if he wanted to hear more. The last thing he wanted was for something to come between them right when they were finding their way back.

"I'll stop if you don't want to hear more."

Michael searched his heart. Did he want to know? Yes, he did. So far, he wasn't creeped out or feeling betrayed. In fact, he was a little flattered Gavin had done so much to get close to him again. "Don't stop," Michael begged.

He felt Gavin smile against his throat. "You asked for it. After a few months, I finally had you telling me a few personal details, and I realized we knew some of the same people. I started finding ways to spend more and more time with those people, hoping to run into you. Then, you showed up at Kieran's house. My patience paid off."

Michael tried to think of something to say but couldn't. The moment he'd realized #1HatTrick was Gavin, Gavin could've tried lying, but he hadn't. He owned up to everything. Michael was a bit twisted when it came to Gavin. He wanted to be the man's crazy obsession. It warmed his insides.

"Are you mad at me?"

Gavin's question came out sounding so insecure, there was no way Michael could get angry. "I always knew there was something about #1HatTrick. He felt too much like a real friend even though we'd never met. I'm not surprised it's you. You've always been the same—too much like a real friend, no matter what."

"We're more than friends," Gavin said with the confidence of a man who hadn't been asleep only moments earlier. "You're mine and I'm yours. If you run, I'll chase you."

Happiness ripped through Michael's chest. He'd waited years to hear those exact words. No way would he let a little bit of stalking stop him from getting everything he wanted from Gavin.

CHAPTER SIX

*G*avin: *What are you doing today?*

Michael: *I have to work.*

Gavin: *That makes sense. Have fun.*

Michael: *What are you doing?*

Gavin: *Nothing. Being bored, I guess.*

Michael: *Would you like to spend the day with me?*

Gavin: *I thought you were working?*

Michael: *Mara won't care if you go with me.*

Gavin: *I'd love that.*

Michael: *You don't even know what I'm doing.*

Gavin: *Don't care. We'll be together.*

Michael: *I'll be there in 15.*

"I can't believe this is what you get paid to do."

Michael rescued the loaf of bread Gavin had been

swinging for the past five minutes and set it in the shopping cart. "This isn't all that I do, by any means, but yeah. It's an amazing job. Mara can't do things like this for herself. She'd get mobbed. At the very least, everyone would snap pictures of everything in her cart and say she hated animals, was sick, or some other stupid shit. So, I do this stuff for her."

Gavin checked the list and grabbed the next item. "So, is she like trapped in her house all the time?"

Michael flashed him a smile. "Not at all. She has a bodyguard. For the most part, she does whatever she wants. Well," Michael paused and seemed think things over before speaking again. "I'm not one hundred percent sure Cal is still on the payroll, but he still takes her everywhere."

"Who's Cal? You lost me," Gavin said as he took control of the cart while Michael went after some fruit.

Michael shrugged as he carried a bag of oranges back to the cart. "He used to be her bodyguard. I don't know." He chewed on his bottom lip and eyed Gavin, looking helpless. "I'm not really in a place to give my opinion on the matter," Michael finally said. "You'll see when you meet them in a few."

Gavin missed a step. "Wait. I'm meeting them?"

"Well, yeah," Michael said with a snort. "Where did you think we were headed with this stuff?"

Gavin realized how stupid his reaction had been. Of course they'd have to take Mara's groceries to her house. "Sorry, I guess I thought she either wouldn't be there or I would never see her if she was."

Michael kissed him on the cheek before wiping it away. "She's been dying to meet you."

It was funny how the idea of meeting Mara King didn't thrill him as much as having Michael freely kissing him did. His heart had been stolen by this man.

"After hearing you talk so highly of her, I'm thrilled. When do I get to take you home?"

Michael's laughter warmed his heart. "It's up to Mara. She might send me to do something else, keep me there for hours, or send me home to work from there. Mara isn't known for being organized. That's what she has me for."

"If you're her keeper, when do I get to take you home?" Gavin knew he was being a pain. He just didn't care. The look Michael shot him had Gavin biting back laughter. Words lodged in his throat. Confessions Michael wasn't ready to hear, but Gavin wanted to give. "I love being with you, wherever we are," Gavin said instead, hoping he could make the words suffice.

Michael moved closer. His expression was the same one the man always wore before getting on his knees. Gavin went hard. Anyone who dared to look would know how hot he was for this man.

"I love being with you too," Michael said, sounding every bit as turned on as Gavin.

Damn, he hoped Mara sent Michael home to work. Gavin didn't think he'd make it long without touching Michael all the ways he craved.

———

Mara fell in love with Gavin and wouldn't let them leave. Cal hadn't been there, stealing Michael's chance to get Gavin's opinion on their relationship. They were such an odd pairing. Michael had hoped Gavin would get a chance to weigh in. Mara had met the man's parents a few months earlier, and tabloids were still blowing up with opinions on the matter. It was also only a matter of time before they realized Mara was pregnant. Once that happened, Michael wouldn't get any rest. Luckily, Mara hadn't tried hiding her pregnancy from Gavin. Now Michael could finally talk to someone about it. It was eating him alive to discuss Cal becoming a father. The man was only half tamed. Hell, he'd once smashed one of Michael's phones.

They'd finally made it back to Michael's ten

minutes ago. Michael fought the urge to crow with relief. Not touching Gavin all day was killing him. The moment they were alone, Michael lost the battle to run his hands up Gavin's chest and draw the man closer. The man's body was beyond amazing, but that wasn't why Michael couldn't resist touching Gavin. Michael couldn't get close enough to satisfy his heart. It ached for more—like a greedy bastard. Gavin leaned against Michael's kitchen counter, where he'd stopped to drink some water, only to be attacked by Michael. He watched Michael though hooded eyes, taunting Michael with his sexy stare. Michael swore the man dared him with his flashing gaze to make a move. Blow his mind. Michael intended to do just that.

"I could get used to the way you're looking at me right now."

Michael didn't pretend not to know how he looked. He didn't doubt for a second everything he felt was on his face. Since he couldn't say the words he wanted, Michael's hands went to Gavin's belt. "I need to taste you," Michael confessed as he touched his lips to the center of Gavin's chest and unzipped the man's pants.

"We should find a better spot," Gavin said, attempting to move away.

Michael wasn't having it. He leaned in to Gavin, keeping the man in place. Gavin was stronger than him. If the man intended to move, Michael couldn't stop him, but he had other ways. Michael set Gavin's cock free. He stroked, enjoying the way the man went hard in his hands. A loud pant filled the kitchen. Michael dropped to his knees, determined to hear the noise again. Gavin's fingers dove into Michael's hair as Michael licked him from root to tip. He toyed with Gavin's slit with his tongue, silently begging for the man's pre-cum. Michael craved that salt like he needed air. That was what Gavin was to him. A necessity to live.

Michael's gaze lifted as he sucked Gavin between his lips. Gavin stared down at him with enough heat to have Michael's dick leaking in his jeans. He felt more than desired. Gavin looked crazed with obsession. Michael wanted that. He needed to keep Gavin right there. Michael held Gavin's stare as he bobbed on the man's cock. In that moment, Gavin belonged to him and no one else. That was what Michael wanted full-time—to own Gavin. He had everything else.

"Michael," Gavin gasped as he openly fucked Michael's mouth. "Damn. You're killing me. I want to bend you over this sink and fuck you like you deserve, but I can't stop. You're too fucking perfect."

Michael took the man down his throat and squeezed, determined to have his cum. Gavin could fuck him later. Michael massaged his own erection through his jeans, trying to ease the building ache.

"You're so goddamn sexy," Gavin said, sounding choked.

Michael toyed with the man's crown, licking away the pre-cum and savoring Gavin's flavor. The man's words spurred him on. Gavin tightened his grip on Michael's hair and pivoted his hips, taking his pleasure. "That's right, baby. There's no one like you." A cry escaped Gavin and hot cum hit the back of Michael's throat. He swallowed. Semen and saliva dripped from his chin. Michael didn't try wiping it away. Instead, he lapped away as much as he could, hoping to hang on to this moment.

Gavin pulled his shirt up and over his head before using it to clean Michael's face. He pulled Michael to his feet. The man's expression stayed the same, as if enthralled by Michael. An ache began in the center of Michael's chest and spread outward. He didn't want Gavin to leave. It was a ridiculous sentiment. The man had a home and a job. Michael didn't care how insane the idea seemed. He wanted to keep Gavin. Michael ground his back teeth to keep from saying anything. He'd never been more scared of opening his mouth and having his emotions pour out.

"I say we take a shower."

Michael nodded. Everything looked slightly out of focus. He was hanging on by a thread. "I'd like that."

Gavin didn't move right away. Instead, he slowly lowered his head, holding Michael's gaze for every moment until their lips met. Michael clung to his wide shoulders. His feet left the floor, and for a second, Michael felt like he was flying before he realized Gavin had swept him into his arms. With one final brush of lips on lips, as if savoring Michael, Gavin headed down the hall. Michael stared at Gavin's set features and did something he hadn't done in years. He prayed. He silently pleaded with God and the universe for this time to be different. No matter the lies he told himself, Michael knew the truth. Gavin had never lost Michael's heart. He'd stolen it six years ago and held on to it tight. There was no one else out there for Michael. He feared there never would be.

———

Gavin swiped some chalk across the canvas, shading in a few areas. His mind fixed upon his work. Michael's birthday was right around the corner and Gavin had to get this finished before then. Michael had some errands to run for Mara and then he'd be back. Gavin didn't have much time alone to get some work done. He was sneaking around his time with Michael to work on the piece as often as he could, but he didn't get many chances. A loud thump of shoes coming down the stairs pulled Gavin from his intense focus, reminding him a real world still existed. A smile grew. Only one person didn't knock. His smile fell. Fuck. He couldn't let Michael see his present. His gaze shot around the room. There was nothing. Half a second before he got busted, Gavin ripped his shirt up and over his head, and tossed it over the canvas.

"Don't be mad," Michael said without preamble.

Gavin tried to act as if he hadn't been seconds away from a full-blown heart attack. "Wow, I get the feeling I'm about to be mad." He pressed a quick kiss to Michael's lips. "I doubt it. It would take a lot to make me upset with you."

Michael took a deep breath as if bracing himself for Gavin's anger. "Mara sent me over to the set of this superhero spoof movie that's in the works to drop off something for her. While I was waiting to speak to the guy I'd been sent to see, I overheard them talking about how they need artwork for the set. See, instead of working for a newspaper, this spoof character draws comics," Michael explained, obviously getting sidetracked. "Anyhow, they want the walls plastered with fake superhero comic book characters. Plus, they need fake comic book sketches for props. For licensing purposes, they can't use just anything. I spoke up and said I knew the perfect guy. Long story short, you've got the job if you want it."

A smile exploded across Gavin's face. "Why would that make me mad?"

Michael shrugged, still looking worried. "You said if you had to find a way to make money from your art, it might kill your love for it. I'd be thrilled for you to do this, but I don't want to kill your love for it. But you can't play hockey forever. This might get your foot in the door."

Gavin hauled Michael against him. "Baby, this is the sweetest thing anyone has ever done for me. With that said, I doubt I'd have time to do it, and hockey isn't a bad paying gig. Shayne played for years—"

"Their budget for the artwork is a hundred and twenty-five thousand," Michael said, cutting him off.

Gavin blinked. "Where do I sign up? I can make the time." Another thought hit him. "Why are you so good to me?"

Michael's expression turned heated as he sidled closer. "Because you're the best part of my day, and I need to make you smile."

Even though Michael's words were sweet, and he was looking at Gavin in a way that made Gavin very happy, Gavin felt his smile slipping away. "Thank you. No one has ever done anything so amazing for me, but I think I should pass."

Michael stepped back out of his hold, looking crestfallen. "What? Why?"

Gavin's chest hurt. He wanted that job with something akin to desperation, but not at the cost of Michael. "You have a lot of amazing connections that I would've never had a shot at meeting without you. I don't want you to wake up one day and decide I used you if I take that job."

"That's stupid," Michael said, sounding pissed. "There's no way I could've known I'd accidentally stumble across this today. You definitely couldn't have known I could or would've been in the right place at the right time. In truth, I never realized jobs like this one exist or I would've suggested it sooner. If you want this job and don't take it because of me, I'll never forgive you."

Despite the rage on Michael's face, a smile exploded across Gavin's. Michael was amazing. "Okay. If it that's important to you, I'll take it."

"Damn right, you will," Michael grumbled as he moved in close once more, wrapping his arms around Gavin's neck. "Now you'll make this moment of ridiculousness up to me by calling Angelo right now and telling him you'll get started right away."

Evil rose inside Gavin. "Will I?" he asked as he grabbed a handful of Michael's ass and pulled him closer, ensuring Michael felt the way he'd gone hard for him. "What if I have other plans for the immediate future instead?"

Michael visibly took a breath, and a flush appeared on his cheeks. In Gavin's head, he was already lifting Michael onto his art table and stripping him bare. "You have ten minutes to make good on whatever you're picturing in your head right now," Michael said, sounding breathless before adding, "and then I expect you to make that call."

"Yes, sir," Gavin said as he captured Michael's mouth. He couldn't do everything he wanted in ten minutes, but he could damn well try. He didn't waste any time lifting Michael off his feet and taking him to the floor. They pulled and tugged at each other's clothes until they were stripped bare. It seemed as if their mouths barely left each other's skin in the process.

The sounds coming from Michael drove Gavin insane. He shifted onto his knees and searched between the recliner and wall for the condoms and lube they'd stashed there earlier in the week. With a condom in place and his fingers coated in lube, Gavin was back kissing Michael in record time. He needed to hear Michael moan. Michael writhed beneath him as Gavin stretched the man's asshole with his lubed fingers. Gavin's plan had been to take Michael hard. The moment his fingers were buried in the man's ass, pushing the button that had Michael crying out against his mouth, Gavin couldn't fucking stop. His dick screamed to feel Michael's tight heat squeezing it. Gavin's heart demanded Michael's pleasure. The way that Michael kissed him — like he was the man's world — Gavin couldn't stop. Michael's hips lifted as he openly fucked Gavin's fingers. Gavin tore his mouth away and gasped for air. He was so goddamn horny, he thought his mind would snap. He waited until he couldn't stand another second before impaling Michael with his cock.

"Oh, god," Michael cried, jacking his erection between them.

Gavin licked and sucked at Michael's neck as he pounded the man's ass. He was crazed with lust and lost in the moment. Words left him with no thought or plan. "Fuck, Michael. You drive me insane. I love being inside you. You're fucking perfect on my dick. This tight ass milks me fucking dry. Goddamn. Give me everything."

Michael's muscles tensed. His ass squeezed Gavin's dick so hard Gavin saw stars. A cry filled the air and Michael's ass spasmed around Gavin's cock, sucking an orgasm from him. Gavin squeezed his eyes closed and clenched his teeth until he thought he'd crack a tooth. Time stopped. Everything fell away. Nothing existed but the two of them and the pleasure rocking his soul.

He collapsed on top of Michael, doing his best not to squash the man. Once he could breathe properly, he rolled to his side and used Michael's shirt to clean away the mess between them before holding Michael to his chest. He couldn't stop touching Michael everywhere he could reach.

"I have a confession," Michael said against his chest.

Gavin ran his fingers through Michael's hair. "Okay."

"In Shreveport, Maksim said New York has been after you for a while. When I heard about that art department job, I hoped it would give you a reason to stay. Now I feel like a bad person. I just want you to be happy."

Defeat sounded heavy in Michael's voice, making Gavin's chest hurt. Gavin didn't need another reason to stay. Hell would freeze before he moved away from Michael. He rearranged their bodies where he could hold Michael's stare. "Baby, I was already happy. Hockey isn't my dream." Michael was. "It's a sport I enjoy that keeps me in shape and makes me money. If they told me tomorrow they didn't have a place for me on the team, I'd be fine. You're not a bad person. In fact," Gavin said, forcing Michael onto his back and covering the man with his body. "You feel pretty damn good to me," Gavin said, running his hands over every inch of Michael he could reach. Michael jumped when Gavin obviously hit a ticklish spot. Gavin did it again, this time digging his fingers in. Michael shoved his hands away and tried squirming away. "Oh, no. I've found a hotspot. You're in trouble now."

Michael flipped onto his stomach and tried to get away. "No." His denial was barely understandable through his laughter.

Gavin used his weight against Michael, pinning him to the floor. "Oh, yes. This is happening."

Michael's entire body shook with silent laughter. "No."

Giving in, Gavin flattened himself against Michael, making it impossible for the man to get away while ensuring he didn't crush him. Love filled him to overflowing. He touched his lips to the shell of Michael's ear while Michael tried catching his breath. "I didn't need another reason to stay," Gavin whispered, incapable of ignoring the emotions raging through him. "You give me one every day when you wake up as mine."

Michael reached behind him and grabbed Gavin's hand and held on. Otherwise, he didn't respond, but he didn't need to. The connection between them went beyond words.

CHAPTER SEVEN

March...

Gavin: *Do you know why I got an invitation to Mara's baby shower?*

Michael: *Because I sent it to you. She doesn't have any family or female friends. It'll be a bunch of guys.*

Gavin: *That's unique, but if you'll be there, so will I. You'll just have to tell me what I'm supposed to do. I've never been to a baby shower.*

Michael: *I've never thrown one. We'll figure it out together.*

———

"Happy birthday," Gavin said at the top of his voice the instant Michael answered his door. "A day early," he added as he used the large bags he carried to push his way inside.

"Thank you. What's all this?"

Gavin could hear the happiness in Michael's voice. He wanted more. "It's a one-man surprise birthday party," Gavin said, dumping everything on Michael's kitchen table. "I have presents, dinner, and some other stuff. I also brought my luggage for my trip tomorrow so I can stay with you every second until it's time for my flight. It's still in the car. I'll bring it in later."

Michael's arms encircled his waist from behind. He pressed his lips to the spot between Gavin's shoulder blades. Gavin's eyes fell closed. He breathed in the moment. Every time Michael kissed him, it was like the man was choosing him all over again. The sensation never got old.

"You're amazing," Michael said against his back.

The tightness in Gavin's chest increased. "Only because you are," Gavin argued. "Now," he said, tugging Michael closer to the table. "Open your presents."

"Oooh, what'd I get?"

Gavin handed him a bright blue bag. It was heavy

and huge. He was ridiculously excited to see Michael's reaction. "Jesus, it's heavy." Michael peered inside as he made the claim. His face lit and the pressure sitting on Gavin's chest increased. After setting the bag on the floor, Michael pulled the first framed watercolor from the bag. Gavin obsessed over the man's every reaction. He watched Michael's gaze move over the piece. "It's us. It's beautiful," Michael said, choking on the last word.

Gavin's throat tightened. "Both pictures are the same," Gavin admitted before Michael could pull out the second. "The other one is glass. There's this service where you can get your artwork scanned and then etched into glass. I didn't know which copy you'd like the most, so I got both. This way, you can choose which one you think goes best with wherever you want to put it."

A line appeared between Michael's brows. "I want them both."

Gavin's smile grew. "They're both yours to do with as you please."

Michael's bright grin reappeared. "I plan to hang them side by side. This is truly gorgeous. I'm amazed at the detail. It's like you painted it while watching us in a mirror."

Gavin's gaze dropped to the image of him kissing

Michael's nape. Fuck, he loved that spot. "I don't need to be in a gallery," Gavin said, prying the picture from Michael's hands. "I'll be in your bedroom. That's better."

"Fuck that," Michael said, taking the frame back. "You'll be hanging over my couch, but later," he said, slipping the painting back in the bag. "Right now, you need to kiss me."

Gavin didn't waste any time wrapping Michael in his arms and capturing his mouth. He wanted everything at once. Gavin craved having Michael tell him about his day. He needed the man to spend the rest of the night kissing him. His body screamed for Gavin to fuck Michael on the table. Gavin didn't know which direction to go. It didn't help that Michael smelled amazing.

Gavin's palm hit the edge of the table, making him realize he'd already backed Michael against it, as if leaning toward fucking him on it. He backed away a hair, trying to slow things down. It was Michael's birthday. He deserved to be celebrated. Gavin needed to get his head out of the sex clouds. "I have one more gift for you," Gavin said between kisses.

Michael's lips shaped into a smile against his. "Is it a dick in a box?"

A snort escaped Gavin. "Now that you've given

me an idea for your next birthday." He tried pulling away. Michael's arms tightened around his neck. He hugged Gavin close. Gavin stroked his back. "What is it?"

"You said that like you plan to be around for my next one."

Gavin pried Michael's arms loose, forcing him back enough he could hold the man's stare. "I don't know what you think this is, but I think you should know by now we're in this for the long haul."

Michael's expression was soft and sweet. "Okay."

Gavin bit the inside of his cheek to keep from laughing. He was so in love with this amazing man. Only a dumbass would think this was temporary. "Time to get your other gift," Gavin urged, leading him from the kitchen.

"Oh my god. It is sex," Michael squealed, sounding like an excited girl.

Gavin grabbed his ribs. Michael cracked him up when he acted ridiculous. "Would you come on?" Michael didn't respond, but he let Gavin tow him outside. Gavin popped the back hatch on his SUV before stepping aside for Michael to see.

"Is that what I think it is?"

Gavin puffed out his chest. "Yep."

"You've got to be fucking shitting me."

"Nope," Gavin said, grabbing the two-person bean bag from the back. "It's our new gaming chair."

"I'm speechless," Michael said, sounding like he really was.

"It'll be great. I promise. Come see," Gavin said, carrying the bulky piece back to the house, trying not to laugh. Michael looked horrified. The chair was way out of style for the man's million-dollar home. Everything Michael owned looked like it had been handpicked by a designer to create the perfect atmosphere for each room. Michael most likely didn't understand. Not yet. Gavin would make him understand. He was about to molest Michael in this chair. It was an old fantasy he was about to make true. Gavin didn't drop the chair until they were inside Michael's den. He plopped down, sinking in before patting his lap for Michael to join him.

"I thought this was our gaming chair."

"It is," Gavin assured him. "Get your phone out before you sit." Michael dug his phone from his pocket and then climbed into Gavin's lap. Gavin's heart swelled as he settled Michael back against his chest. "Open our game. Let's finish building that new research center."

Michael did as he bade while Gavin watched over his shoulder. "I like this," Michael said as if admitting a dirty secret.

He had no idea Gavin was just getting started.

"What about dinner?"

Fuck. Gavin would need to move quick. He'd forgotten their dinner was getting cold in the kitchen. "It'll hold for a few minutes while you test drive this new chair."

Michael nodded as he readjusted his position, ensuring Gavin could see what he was doing in the Cyborg game.

Gavin's hands slid from Michael's waist to the button of his jeans. He felt more than heard Michael take a deep breath. Gavin slipped the button loose and slid Michael's zipper down. Michael didn't try stopping him.

"I'm addicted to the way you smell," Gavin said against the side of Michael's neck as he dove inside Michael's jeans. Michael tossed the phone aside, giving up any pretense of paying attention to the game. Instead, he gripped Gavin's knees and held on as Gavin stroked his cock. "I want to have you the way you have me."

"You've got me," Michael said, sounding breathless and lifting his hips to meet Gavin's fist.

Gavin wasn't sure that was true, but they were on their way and he needed Michael to burn alive in his arms. He needed it to be his hands that brought Michael to the edge of insanity before pushing him over. Maybe then Michael would know a second of what it was like inside Gavin's head every hour of every day. "You'll come for me," Gavin promised. "And then we'll enjoy our dinner before I fuck you on your overly expensive kitchen table."

Michael made a choking sound.

A smile that felt evil even to him twisted Gavin's lips. "Then I have cake," Gavin added before opening his mouth over the side of Michael's neck and sucking. He handled Michael's cock the same as he would his own and swore the pleasure was his. His dick cried for attention, but it was a muted desire behind the screaming of his heart. That organ wanted Michael's love and he wouldn't stop until Michael was sick with the need to be with Gavin.

Michael writhed in his hold. His rapid breathing spoke volumes about how close he was to orgasm. "Gavin." Michael's muscles stiffened.

Gavin cupped Michael's jaw and tilted the man's head back so he could capture his mouth. He sucked on Michael's bottom lip as he sent the man over the edge. Hot cum coated his fingers. He didn't stop stroking Michael's dick even when the man had nothing left to give. Gavin wasn't ready to break the connection. Michael tasted too good—felt too good in his arms.

"I fucking love this chair," Michael said against his lips.

"I knew you would," Gavin said before going back to kissing him. Gavin had a list of mundane things in his head he intended to make amazing because they enjoyed them together. By his calculations, it would take them forever to check off each one.

———

Time always slipped away faster than Michael liked when he was with Gavin. They'd spent one hell of a night together. Unfortunately, their time was almost up. Soon, Gavin would be on a plane headed for Montreal for his next game and Marshall would be there so they could celebrate their birthday together.

As if thoughts of giving up his time alone with Gavin conjured him, Marshall came through the front door without knocking—like always. They were beyond boundaries. Michael treated Marshall's house the same.

"Happy birthday," Marshall called as he barreled into the kitchen, carrying several grocery bags. "Steaks and all the fixings, as promised," he said, setting the bags on the counter. If he was the least bit surprised to see Gavin, he didn't mention it. Instead, he dipped his chin at Gavin. "What's up?" Without waiting for a response, he grabbed Michael in a bear hug, lifting his feet from the floor. "Twin!"

Michael slapped him across the back and prayed oxygen came back to his brain. "Gavin's already dragged the grill from the garage for you."

"Yeah?" Marshall asked, tossing a quick glance Gavin's way. "There's enough for three. You staying?"

"He was just about to head out," Michael answered for him, because Gavin looked uncomfortable beneath Marshall's stare. He'd known this moment would come. Until now, he'd managed to avoid any contact between the two. Since they both played sports that had games around Thanksgiving and Christmas, they'd made it through the holidays without having to be in the same place. If Gavin was serious about the long haul, they couldn't dodge each other forever.

Gavin nodded. "I'm on my way out," he said, mimicking Michael's words.

Marshall's disapproval was so thick it was almost tangible. "It's your man's birthday and you're headed out of town. Nice," Marshall said, still smiling, but getting his dig in.

Gavin didn't stop smiling either. It was like they were challenging each other's ability to play nice. "If you had a game today, that's where'd you be. I don't have a choice. There's a game. I have to be there."

Michael jumped in, hoping to make the silent pissing contest end. "It's just a date on a calendar. We can celebrate anytime. Plus, he's already given me my present. Look," Michael said, fetching the paintings where he'd left them on the kitchen table. He handed them over. "Gavin made them for me. Aren't they amazing?"

"I didn't know you painted," Marshall said, inspecting the canvas boards.

Michael's mouth fell open. "You were his best friend for years. How did you not know that?"

Marshall shrugged and set the paintings aside. "Anyhow, I brought some steaks. You care if I go ahead and fire up the grill? I'm starving."

Michael nodded, setting Marshall free from a conversation he obviously didn't want to have, but he was still reeling. If Marshall knew Gavin at all, he should've known that. He glanced Gavin's way. Gavin didn't look upset or offended.

Gavin winked once they were alone. "I guess it could've gone worse, but maybe it's a good thing I have a flight to catch."

"Thank you for trying. I'm sorry things are so awkward. Hopefully, they'll get better with time."

Gavin shrugged and pulled Michael into his arms. "It's hard to make me uncomfortable. He'll get used to having me around, and if he doesn't, it doesn't change anything. I'd still rather be with you than anywhere else in the world, even if Marshall glares at me the whole time."

Michael chewed his bottom lip, biting back a smile. All he ever did was smile anymore, and it was all Gavin's fault. "Kiss me before Marshall gets back," Michael whispered.

Gavin's eyes flashed with devilry as he boxed Michael in against the counter. He moved slow, driving Michael insane. Finally, he dipped his head and touched his lips to Michael's. "Mine," Gavin mouthed against Michael's lips so quietly Michael felt more than heard it.

"Damn, I'll miss you this weekend." The admission was out of Michael's control.

A throat cleared behind them, and Gavin straightened away. His gaze remained locked on Michael. His lips twisted into a wicked smile that had Michael pressing his hand against his stomach to quell the butterflies.

"I guess I'd better grab my bags." Gavin backed away as he made the claim.

On a sigh, Michael switched his gaze Marshall's way and set Gavin free. Marshall shot him a look Michael couldn't read, but he got the impression it was disapproval. Since Michael didn't care to see it, he watched Gavin make his way down the hall. Damn, he loved watching Gavin's body move.

"You've got it bad," Marshall muttered as he dug through Michael's silverware drawer.

It wasn't like Michael could deny it. "Do you need any help?"

"Just see your man off," Marshall said, shooting him another dark look before heading back outside to the grill.

With a weary sigh, Michael went looking for Gavin. He couldn't fix everything, but being with Gavin fixed everything for him. "Do you have everything ready to go?" Michael asked as he cleared the door.

Gavin overcame him, snatching him off the floor into a bear hug. A loud laugh escaped Michael. It was as if only a few minutes in Marshall's company had already turned Gavin into the fool he'd been back when he'd been Marshall's best friend. He pressed several noisy kisses to the side of Michael's neck before releasing him. "Okay. Stop playing around. I have to go. Dang."

Michael shook his head at Gavin's ridiculousness. "Kiss me and go, then," Michael said, using the same put-out tone as Gavin.

Gavin's expression turned serious. Michael's heart turned over in his chest. The distance between them disappeared. Their mouths collided. Michael's throat swelled at the sweetness of their kiss. In times like these, he caught glimpses of their future together, and it looked beautiful. Gavin's tongue moved against his. Michael clung to his wide shoulders, feeling small and protected.

"I'll call you as soon as I'm settled," Gavin promised as he pulled away.

Michael nodded, incapable of speech. He followed Gavin down the hall and to the front door, fighting the urge to follow him all the way to the airport. Sometimes it sucked being an adult. He had to suck it up and watch Gavin go.

When Gavin was gone, and the door shut tight behind him, Michael turned to find Marshall watching him. Concern etched his brother's every feature. Michael comforted himself that Marshall had —at least—waited until they were alone.

"So, Gavin Weeks... again."

Michael flashed him a smile and moved to sit on one of the barstools at the bar, separating the kitchen from the living room. "Seems so."

"Why?" Marshall asked without preamble before attempting to backtrack when he obviously heard the same condemnation in his tone that Michael did. "I mean, in high school, I could kind of see it. Despite all his bullshit slurs and denying you in public, he wasn't good at hiding the way he looked at you. It was always as if the rest of the world disappeared. That's why I never got mad for real when he would call you a homo or whatever, because I knew he didn't mean it, and you never acted as if it bothered you much. I thought you had things under control. That's why I didn't speak up about a lot of things." Marshall snagged a stool from the bar and pulled it closer, while still holding Michael's gaze. "Like I said, I get why you let shit go on back then. What I don't understand is why you'd willingly choose to take him back now, after all the things he's done."

Michael wasn't offended. In fact, it warmed his heart that Marshall cared. He was the only person Michael could speak to about any of this. No one else cared to hear it or knew all the details of their past. That was why Michael didn't hesitate being honest. "For one thing, it was a long time ago. I can't lie and say it doesn't still sting when I think about that night and Zoey, but his family isn't like ours. He was scared of being like me. I get that. My life hasn't been easy."

Marshall's disapproving expression didn't falter. "It wasn't just Zoey. She was only one of many girls." Michael's stomach twisted at Marshall's words, but Marshall wasn't finished. "And you weren't the only guy, so don't tell me he was hiding or scared."

It took every ounce of Michael's willpower to

keep breathing. Marshall's words hurt more than Michael could've dreamed. He'd known—sort of—about the girls. They were cover. But other guys, Michael couldn't take it. That meant he wasn't special, only convenient. What about now? Was that what he was now—convenient? "That's the first I've heard of other guys," Michael said, hearing how tight his voice had gone.

Marshall looked uncomfortable—like he regretted bringing it up, but it was too late. The words were spoken, never to be unheard. "Really, it was just one other guy." Marshall hesitated again, making Michael want to shake him before he spoke up and shattered Michael's heart. "Me."

The air left Michael's lungs in a whoosh. If it had been Marshall's intention to break him, he'd succeeded. Michael couldn't breathe past the betrayal. "What?" Even Michael heard the panic in his question. How could Gavin come back into his life after that? "What?" he repeated, sounding closer to an enraged roar this time than a question.

Marshall looked panicked now that he seemed to realize his confession had hit home. He scrambled to explain. "We only made out—like kissing, but I thought you knew. I thought—surely—he would've told you everything by now."

"No," Michael growled. "No one has ever told me

shit. Including you." Just made out? It was his fucking twin. The better twin, at that. How could they have kissed? David's claims had been true that night. He was the one Gavin had settled for because he couldn't have Marshall.

Marshall stood. "I shouldn't have said anything. You looked happy with him, and that was a long time ago. I thought you knew," he added, sounding helpless. "You're my brother, Michael," Marshall finished lamely.

That added a whole new level of betrayal to the mix. They were brothers. "In one breath, you say you knew about us, and in another, you admit to being the other guy. I'm just..." Michael stared at Marshall, feeling attacked from all sides. "I don't understand."

The devastation in Marshall's eyes was the only thing keeping Michael sane. "I wasn't like you," Marshall said with heartbreak etching every word. "I'm not like you," Marshall restated. "I'm not brave enough to endure the way you do. Back then, being normal meant everything to me. I didn't want to want him, but you did. That's why I stepped back and pretended not to know. That's why I kept playing the part I'd set for myself. The one I keep setting for myself. You get to be you. Always have." The more Marshall spoke, the more Michael's heart broke. He wished his brother wouldn't choose this life in the closet, but he understood. It wasn't easy to be him, and he didn't have the world looking at him the way Marshall did. But the way Marshall sounded—like there was no air—Michael didn't want that for him. "I never would've hurt you," Marshall said, and Michael couldn't doubt him. Marshall wasn't that guy. He always smiled and made everyone else laugh. It broke Michael's heart, because Marshall was miserable inside where no one could see.

"I know," Michael finally said, setting Marshall free of his guilt. Too bad it didn't help Michael's heart. He'd been certain he'd been meant for Gavin, and that was why they'd found their way back to each other. Now it felt like another of life's cruel jokes. Michael had no clue how he'd handle this. He stood. "I guess I should start the salad while you cook. We won't turn twenty-four again. Have you heard from Mom and Dad?"

"They're in St. Martin. Michael."

At the sound of his name, Michael finally met Marshall's gaze. He tried for a smile. "It's okay. I've always been alone, right?"

Marshall growled. "I didn't mean to fuck things up."

The thing was—Michael wasn't so sure that was true, but he didn't have the energy to fight. "Go cook. It's fine."

With one last defeated look, Marshall finally went back outside. Michael went through the motions of chopping all the vegetables Marshall had brought. He kept his mind carefully blank. Right now, he couldn't picture Gavin kissing Marshall, whispering secrets to him in the dark. He couldn't be the second choice again. Michael just couldn't.

CHAPTER EIGHT

*G*avin: *I'm safely on the ground.*

   Gavin: *Judging by your radio silence, I'm guessing you're out partying with Marshall.*

Gavin: *Did you make it home last night?*

Gavin: *Okay, now I'm getting worried. Please answer my calls or at least text me and let me know you're still alive,*

Gavin: *Seriously, are you dead in a ditch somewhere?*

#1HatTrick: *You around?*

This user does not exist.

Gavin: *I'm guessing, since you've deleted your gaming account that you're alive and we just have some problem I don't understand. You could at least be a man and tell me what I've done.*

Gavin: *I'm coming to Mara's baby shower. If you don't want me there, I'd suggest you answer my calls and tell me.*

Michael kept shooting him dirty looks from across the room and Gavin had never been more lost. He had no fucking clue what happened. When he'd left for Montreal, they'd been perfect. The second he'd left, everything had gone to hell with no explanation. Gavin had a bad feeling in the pit of his stomach that Marshall was to blame.

He didn't want to be angry, but Gavin was enraged. The first time Michael had walked away from him without a word, there had been a clear-cut reason and it had been Gavin's fault. This time around, Gavin had no fucking clue what was going on. He wanted to cross the room and shake Michael. It took every ounce of his self-control not to make the biggest scene of his life.

Mara's house was packed with men Gavin knew from work. Each one had spoken to him. Gavin couldn't remember a fucking word of what was said to him. All he saw was Michael's evil glances. Gavin bided his time. Michael would talk to him today, even if Gavin had to kidnap him. Fucking Marshall. Gavin had left Michael's for the airport with a bad feeling in the pit of his stomach. Now he knew why. If he couldn't work things out with Michael, Gavin would kill Marshall after this. He'd spent the last week hoping he was wrong and something hadn't come between Michael and him. Now, he couldn't avoid the truth. Marshall had said something. Gavin would ruin him. He'd never been more furious. As he looked on, Michael headed for the door. Kieran was in the middle of pitching him a team in New York. Gavin walked away without looking back. He wasn't leaving Michael for any amount of money, and he had bigger problems right now than being rude.

———

Michael felt Gavin's gaze on him throughout the entire shower. Gavin made a few attempts to speak to him, but Michael kept his distance and stayed stuck to Cal's or Mara's side for safety. Despite his dark looks, Michael wasn't scared of Gavin. He was frightened of himself. All it had taken was one look at Gavin in person, and Michael had almost caved. Goddamn, he hated himself for loving Gavin. He hit the door damn near running the instant Mara set him free. Michael couldn't get out from underneath Gavin's stare fast enough. The moment he cleared the door, he knew Gavin followed. The man walked harder than any person Michael had ever met. Michael swore he could feel Gavin stalking him and hear every step he took behind him.

"Why are you doing this, Michael? Why are you ignoring me and shutting me out? I've done everything I can to prove myself."

Michael snapped. It had been the world's longest two hours beneath Gavin's accusing gaze. He spun and closed the distance between them. "Do you know what your problem is?" Michael asked, going toe to toe with Gavin.

Gavin didn't back down an inch. "Bated breath here. The sooner you fucking say it, the faster we can have this out."

Gavin's smartassery rolled off Michael. He'd been angry too long to walk away now. "You make me love you. Every fucking time. And it's not fair, because I'm not who you want." Gavin looked as if Michael had slapped him. That gave Michael pause, but not for long. "Yeah, that's right. Marshall told me about the two of you."

All the anger bled from Gavin's face. "You're so blind," Gavin said, sounding tired. For a moment, he stared at Michael, as if seeing him for the first time. The ugliest snort Michael had ever heard left Gavin. "I'm so stupid I'd laugh if there was a goddamn thing funny about this. All these years, I've been thinking you were the only person who ever saw me, but you're just like everyone else."

The tables turned so fast on Michael, he no

longer knew what was happening, but he had a terrible feeling he was the bad guy. "What do you mean?" Even to Michael's ears, he sounded unsure.

Gavin shook his head and took a step back. His expression had never looked faker—like Gavin had donned a mask—the same one he gave the rest of the world. It was cold on the outside of Gavin. "I've always been mediocre at all the things expected of me. The things I love, I've had to hide. I came around for you," Gavin said, as if Michael should've known. "All those years, for you. Marshall was convenient, and I knew no one would find out, because Hell would freeze before Marshall let anyone know he'd kissed a guy. But it felt wrong. Everything about it was wrong. I didn't want him. He was like me—hiding behind douchery, and I already hated me. That's not what I craved." A bitter smile touched Gavin's lips. "I wanted the dark, weird guy who didn't give a damn what anyone thought. The only time I ever had anything in common with Marshall was when I pretended to be who everyone expected me to be. You were the only one who let me be real. I thought you got that, but I was wrong. Sorry to waste your time," Gavin said before walking away.

Michael didn't move. He stared at the spot where Gavin had been only moments earlier and absorbed every word, searching for any hint of truth. Michael remembered the slurs and the way it felt the night he'd lost Gavin, but he'd forgotten why he'd let that first kiss happen between them. There were other nights before that kiss—times when Gavin had secretly shown him his art. Played video games with him while Marshall made out with some girl. He'd chosen to stay behind with Michael when Marshall wanted to go to parties Michael hadn't been invited to. Gavin had intentionally done things to keep anyone from thinking they were friends, but Michael hadn't felt disliked. Horror struck as quickly as the truth. Gavin had shown up for him in the only way he could under the worst of circumstances for himself. He wasn't like Michael. No one gave Gavin the freedom to be open and proud. His actions reflected on his father and Coach would probably rather die than hear his son was gay. So Gavin had found another way to be with Michael. Did it really matter to him if Gavin kissed Marshall once? Did he care the world hadn't known about them in high school? This whole mess was stupid. He was letting old hurts stop him from having the only person who'd ever gotten under his skin. Gavin deserved better because Michael hadn't lied. He loved Gavin. Always had. All these years, he'd never let him go. Michael didn't intend to start now. He would make this right because Gavin was his.

Michael didn't wait to get started. Procrastination wasn't in his blood. He headed back inside, making a beeline for the only person who could help him. Mara might be a few weeks away from giving birth to twins, but no one got their way the way she did. His desperation must've been written all over his face, because Mara perked up at the first sight of him.

"Have you finally decided to let me help you?" she asked without preamble. She'd known he'd been acting different since Gavin returned to his life, but Michael was a private person. He couldn't afford to keep secrets any longer.

"I need someone who isn't afraid of a little B and E."

Kieran sidled up next to him, obviously overhearing. "I know a Russian who isn't afraid to steal whatever you need, even if it's another person."

Thank God. Kieran Steele was the most ruthless agent in the world. He was exactly the type of person Michael needed. "It's nothing quite as dramatic as kidnapping." He thought it over and added, "yet." But, goddamn it, shit was about to get done, because Michael couldn't live with knowing he'd hurt the man he loved. Gavin would see Michael knew him if it was the last fucking thing Michael did.

———

Too late, Gavin realized Michael had confessed to loving him. He was halfway to wherever unnamed place his SUV carried him before it hit him. Michael had definitely said he loved Gavin. Unfortunately, Gavin's temper had snapped—the way it always did, ruining everything. He did the stupidest things when his heart was engaged. Fucking Michael. Every goddamn time Gavin felt like he was done, Michael gave him a reason to hang on. He couldn't walk away now that Michael had confessed to loving him. Gavin equally didn't know how to fight the past. How long would he have to pay for shit he'd done years ago? He'd been a different person back then.

Michael needed Gavin to claim him in front of the world—without shame. Gavin got that. He'd spent a lot of time denying Michael and humiliating him back then. Michael would never fully forgive him until Gavin fixed all that. And, fuck, that one night with Marshall. That would never stop haunting him. He'd been drunk and stupid. Marshall had been hiding—just like him. Gavin had been staring at Michael and craving for so fucking long, and Marshall had been there. David had been wrong when he'd said Gavin got to stare into Michael's eyes and pretend it was Marshall. It had been the other way around, and also why it hadn't gone farther. No matter how hard he'd tried or drunk he'd been, his heart had known it wasn't Michael beneath him. The next day, he'd given in and kissed Michael. Gavin's heart had never looked back, or forward, for that matter. He would figure this out if it was the last damn thing he did because— goddamn it—he loved Michael. The stubborn ass. Unfortunately, there was only one person who could help him above all others. Gavin only hoped he didn't beat the shit out of him at first glance.

When Gavin reached Marshall's, he beat on the front door with too much enthusiasm while picturing the wooden slab as Marshall's face. The door opened and Marshall eyed him, looking unsurprised to find Gavin standing on his front porch. "Are you here to punch me? You should probably aim for my nose," Marshall said, twisting his fingers, and looking so damn guilty Gavin couldn't even be mad.

"I'm not here to hit you," Gavin said. Even to his ears, he sounded unsure if the words were true.

"I swear, I thought he knew," Marshall said, as he stepped back, silently inviting Gavin inside. "You should've seen his face," he added, sounding like he felt like the worst person on the planet.

Gavin's anger fell away. Instead, he wanted to die. He couldn't imagine Michael's devastation. "It probably looked a lot like he looked at me a few minutes ago when he dumped me," Gavin said as he plopped down on Marshall's love seat, as if he owned the place. "If it had been anyone other than you, he might not have said a word to me about it, but you've always been a sore spot for him."

Marshall's face screwed up in confusion. "What's that supposed to mean?"

Gavin's brow pulled together in thought. There was no way Marshall was that blind. "You're you and he's him."

He could see Marshall's temper spiking. "What the fuck is that supposed to mean? There's not a goddamn thing wrong with my brother."

A smile pulled at Gavin's lips. Despite current circumstances, Marshall was an awesome brother, but then again, he wasn't, because he was blind. "I know that. He's the one I fell in love with, but you've always been popular and he's always been teased. While you played on every team, he stayed home and tried staying out of your way."

"We had parties every weekend," Marshall said, keeping up the argument even though he'd lost some fire.

"*You* had parties. Michael hid, because your friends, myself included, made sure he knew he wasn't welcome. Face it, Marshall, you've always been the golden child. He was just in your shadow, trying to support you."

Marshall threw himself down on the couch across

from Gavin, looking dejected. "And then I told him about us."

"There was no us," Gavin said, determined to make everything right. "I was wrong to ever kiss you. Granted, it happened before anything ever happened with Michael, but I knew it was a mistake. I love him, Marshall. Always have. I'm sorry I was such a shitty friend and an even shittier teenager. But I need you to help me now."

Marshall eyed him, looking wary. "What do you need me to do?"

"Get him to go to tomorrow night's game. I'll get you tickets and take care of everything else. I just need him to be there, so I can make everything right."

Marshall nodded. "He'll be there, even if I have to kidnap him."

A smile tugged at Gavin's lips. "Thank you." Gavin's eyes stung as he stared at Marshall. He really had been Gavin's best friend. It was just another relationship Gavin had fucked up over the years. Goddamn, he was tired. He was trying his ass off, but no one ever noticed.

"You know, my number hasn't changed either," Marshall said, taking him by surprise. "Just in case, you know, you ever want to call or whatever."

Marshall sounded so goddamn uncomfortable Gavin didn't know what to say.

So he smiled. "Maybe I will. You know, sometime."

Looking relieved, Marshall nodded. "Okay. I guess I'll see you tomorrow night."

"Yeah," Gavin said, coming to his feet. Tomorrow night, he'd make things right. He had to. The alternative was unthinkable.

CHAPTER NINE

*M*ichael spent too much time alone with his thoughts, plotting his way back into Gavin's life. Probably, a sane person would've just called or went over to the man's house and begged for forgiveness. The thing was—Gavin deserved more. The man had stalked him via a game for months before making his move. Michael could show Gavin the same level of intensity. He was determined. Everything was set. By the end of the night, Michael would know—either he'd fixed everything, or they'd be done for good. There was no going back from this grand scale of a plan. Michael swiped his hand over his face. He hadn't stopped feeling sick to his stomach since Mara's baby shower. Chances were good he was making the biggest mistake of his life, but he had to try. Michael's phone rang, saving him from the insanity running through his brain. He checked the face. When he spotted Marshall's name, he sucked in a deep breath. Marshall would always be his twin, even if Gavin refused to take Michael back. He couldn't avoid his brother forever.

"Hello?"

"I have a huge favor to ask, and I'm worried with you being on the outs with Gavin, and no doubt— justifiably—pissed off at me, you'll tell me no."

Michael smiled at Marshall's fast-talking mouthful —like he'd half expected Michael to hang up on him before he could get his words out. He was incapable of telling Marshall no. "Hit me. You never know."

"Well, I've got two club level tickets to the Blue Fires game tonight. The team is doing a shout out on the Jumbotron to me, bragging about me being this year's starting quarterback for the Land Sharks. Anyhow, I was hoping you'd go with me."

Michael chewed his bottom lip. If Gavin was playing tonight and Michael was with Marshall, on the Jumbotron no less, no one could claim he'd broken into Gavin's house. Seemed perfect to him. "Would you like me to wear your jersey?"

Marshall's triumphant cry made it worthwhile. "I think you should wear Gavin's."

Michael went back to chewing on his bottom lip. That would be awesome. That is, if Gavin even saw it. "I could do that."

"Awesome," Marshall said, sounding happy. "I'll come by and get you around six, if that's okay?"

"Works for me," Michael agreed even as he mentally rearranged his plans for a home invasion. "I'll see you at six." After exchanging goodbyes, Michael hung up and dialed Kieran's number. He needed to tweak his plan of action.

By the time Marshall arrived, Michael thought he'd crawl out of his skin. He paced the floor and tugged at his clothes, questioning his every decision. He'd worn a long-sleeve t-shirt beneath Gavin's jersey, since the arena would be cold. Right now, he was burning alive.

"You look ready to flip out. Are you sure you want to do this?" Marshall asked, looking concerned.

"Absolutely," Michael said, somehow managing to sound excited. "It's your night. I'm here for you. That's what brothers are for."

"Exactly," Marshall said, sounding a little too enthusiastic. Michael chalked it up to nerves. He was about to face a crowd of thousands after all. Unexpectedly, Marshall pulled him into a hug.

"What's this?" Michael asked, patting him on the back.

"Just thinking," Marshall said as he pulled away. "We don't really look that much alike anymore. That makes me sad."

"Okay," Michael said, dragging out the word. "Are you feeling nostalgic?"

Marshall shrugged. "Like I said, just thinking. It's always been just us. When we were kids, I didn't think about it much. As long as we kept our grades up and cleaned up our parties before Mom and Dad saw them, no one ever paid attention to us."

"Your parties," Michael reminded him.

"Whatever," Marshall said with a laugh. "The point is, all we've ever really had is each other. I guess I'm just happy you're going with me tonight. There's no one else I'd rather have with me."

To Michael's surprise, the backs of his eyes stung at Marshall's confession. They were brothers, and they had all the issues that came along with that, but —in truth—Marshall was his best friend. "Love you, Marsh," Michael said before the moment got away.

"Love you too, Mikey. I'm sorry I'm always failing you."

Marshall looked so damn sincere, the pressure on Michael's chest increased. "You're not. Don't think that again."

Marshall ever-present smile reappeared. He slung one arm around Michael's neck and headed for the door. "Let's go before this turns into a tampon commercial." There was the brother Michael knew and loved. Michael had known he was in there somewhere.

Michael listened to Marshall chatter about game stats and people Michael didn't know all the way to the arena. He made all the appropriate noises to keep up his end, but Michael's brain was stuck in a loop of silent panic. By the time they were club level, Michael was ridiculously happy to see a familiar face just to have a break from the monotony of crazy inside his head.

The smile tugging at the corners of Michael's mouth felt over the top even to him as he pushed his way through the crowd to reach Maksim's side. "Hey," he called, snagging the man's attention.

Maksim turned. His smile was luminous as he greeted Michael. "Hello again. We're getting very good at meeting like this." His gaze slid over Michael's shoulder before meeting Michael's stare again, and then immediately moving back to over his shoulder. "I don't wish to alarm you, but you have a man who looks exactly like you standing right behind you."

Michael snorted. Maksim was exactly the distraction he needed. He moved to the side, making room for Marshall before motioning his brother's way. "Maksim, this is my brother, Marshall. Marshall, Maksim Petrov. He's a talent scout."

Maksim held out his hand for Marshall to shake. "It is nice to meet you. Your face is familiar to me," Maksim said before laughing. "That wasn't meant to be the joke it turned out to be. I honestly believe I've seen you before. In fact, I'm already positive I'd like to see you again."

"Marshall is quarterback for the Land Sharks," Michael explained, hoping to skate past Maksim's flirting before Marshall landed in an uncomfortable position.

"Ah, that explains things. Would the two of you care to sit with me?"

"I'd like that," Marshall said, quietly answering for them.

Michael's gaze shot the man's way. He couldn't remember the last time he'd heard Marshall speak in such a serious tone. His brother was the fun one. Michael was the serious one. That was just how things were. Marshall's usual smile was gone. His gaze remained locked on Maksim, and he moved to follow the man before Michael got a read on Marshall's sudden change in mood.

When they reached Maksim's private table, Michael chose the opposite side, leaving Marshall to sit next to Maksim. Marshall didn't seem bothered.

In fact, he still hadn't stopped staring at the charismatic Russian.

"Where are you from, Mr. Petrov?"

Maksim winked. "It is Maksim only. I am from Samara. It is the sixth largest city in Russia."

Marshall's smile finally made an appearance. "I don't know much about Russia. Sorry."

The way Maksim smiled had Michael leaning forward in his seat. He was dying to know what the man was thinking. Michael had never seen a wickeder grin. "If you'd like to learn, I'd be happy to give you a tour. It is a very beautiful place. Of course, it's cold, and you are probably used to the heat. I'm sure I could find ways to keep you warm."

Marshall played the fool. "I've heard how y'all like to drink."

"Among other things," Maksim said, inching closer to Marshall.

It was odd. The first time Michael met Maksim, he hadn't thought the man especially handsome. As he spoke to Marshall, openly flirting, Michael realized the man was gorgeous. His dark blue eyes were almost violet. They flashed with heat when he stared at Marshall. His dark hair kept falling in his face. Marshall's hand shot out, as if he intended to push a strand behind Maksim's ear. He caught himself and dropped his hand to the table. Michael couldn't look away. He wanted to search the ice for Gavin and eat his man alive with this stare. He loved watching Gavin in action, but Marshall had his attention. His brother was alive in a way Michael had never seen. It was fascinating and had the added benefit of keeping Michael from thinking too much about what was currently taking place at Gavin's. Damn, he hoped no one got arrested tonight.

Shayne appeared at the edge of the table, saving Michael from staring and from worrying. He handed Marshall an ear piece and another to Michael. "Put these in. They'll be announcing you soon."

"Wait," Michael said, holding the ear piece away from him like a snake. "Why do I need this?"

"They'll be highlighting you as well. You're here with Marshall," Shayne said evasively before moving along and leaving Michael floundering behind him.

He looked at Marshall in confusion. "Why do I need this?"

Marshall shrugged. "Just put it in. We're almost out of time." Michael shoved the ear piece in as Marshall appeared on the Jumbotron.

"Joining us tonight, cheering for his home team, is quarterback for the New Orleans Land Sharks, Marshall Frost."

Marshall smiled and waved to the sound of loud cheers—like the star he was born to be.

To Michael's surprise, his image appeared on the large screen. "Also joining us this evening is Marshall's twin, Michael Frost, fiancé to Blue Fires Forward, Gavin Weeks."

Michael waved before the words sank in. The loud clapping and whistling from the surrounding crowd left Michael wondering if he'd heard the announcement in his ear correctly. The camera focused on Gavin, who pumped his fist in the air once, making the noise of the crowd increase by tenfold. Michael could only blink. He had no idea what was happening.

"Congratulations," Maksim said, shaking Michael's hand. Michael let it go on, trying to figure out what just happened to his life.

"Thank you." His numb lips formed the words, even though they didn't make sense. Michael's brain didn't unthaw until Marshall moved around the table and hugged him.

His brother spoke close to his ear. "Stop looking so shocked. People might think you're unhappy. By the way, after what Gavin just did, I'm glad you didn't give up on him through all these years. He obviously loves you and that's all I've ever wanted—someone to deserve you."

"What just happened?" Even Michael could hear the confusion in his voice. "Did you do this?"

Marshall slapped him across the back, managing to still play the part for anyone watching. "Nah. I just got you here. This was all Gavin. He loves you, Michael. You don't have to marry him. He'll be the only one embarrassed if you don't, but hear him out after the game. Dude loves you."

"What are your plans later tonight?" Maksim asked, appearing at Marshall's side and holding a beer out for him. Michael hadn't even realized Maksim had left.

Marshall's expression turned wary and Michael's stomach dropped. "How do you mean?" Marshall asked, his voice tight.

Maksim nodded toward Michael. "Your brother will understandably wish to go home with his fiancé. Perhaps you'd like to go home with me?" Maksim said the words with such confidence, any other man he approached would've easily said yes. Marshall wasn't any man, and Michael forgot his own predicament. A groan rose in his throat and stuck as Marshall's usual fake smile appeared.

He didn't reach for the beer. "I think you have the wrong idea about me."

Maksim's eyebrows rose. He did not have the wrong impression. Everyone standing there knew it. The gorgeous Russian transformed from smooth flirt to cold indifference so quickly Michael got a chill. "I see. You're a coward. How tiresome." Without another word, he walked away.

Marshall's eyes flashed fire at the man's back. "Oh, hell no," he said, going after the man who was quickly disappearing. Michael watched until both men were out of sight. He couldn't fix Marshall's problems and his own right now. Maybe Maksim was exactly what Marshall needed. All Michael knew right now was everyone was saying the m-word around him and he hadn't been asked. In fact, he'd shown up tonight, praying Gavin wasn't finished with him for good while hatching a plan of his own.

His gaze fixed upon the ice where Gavin skated toward the goal. The man was large and powerful. He was soft and beautiful on the inside—where he only let Michael see. Fuck. Michael was ridiculously in love with Gavin. What if the announcers had made a mistake? Surely they'd misread who he was and Gavin would laugh about it after the game... if Gavin even spoke to him after the game.

"Congratulations," Shayne said, reappearing with a tech guy to retrieve the ear piece.

Michael handed it over while dodging Shayne's stare. "Thank you. I think they made a mistake, though."

Shayne's smile never dimmed. "Not at all. Gavin asked me for this favor and I obliged. No mistakes.

Your brother being here is a huge media boost. People love seeing sports teams from their hometown supporting one another. They also like feeling as if they're part of the players' family, which means getting all the big announcements on their personal lives. The Blue Fires are proud to have you joining our family."

Michael couldn't respond. Marshall's claim rang loud in his head. Gavin would be the one embarrassed if Michael denied this. No way would he let that happen. In truth, Michael shouldn't have been that surprised. This was a total Gavin move. He wanted something, so he took it. Just like the first time they'd kissed and the first time he'd slipped inside Michael's bed. When he'd spotted Michael inside that coffee shop, he'd found a way to insert himself back in Michael's life. Despite their need to talk, Michael realized he couldn't stop smiling. It seemed he liked having his life taken over. Plus, Gavin could hardly get mad over Michael's plans now. He couldn't wait to see Gavin's face.

———

Gavin wondered if he'd puke. If Michael didn't show up for him after the game, despite Marshall's plan to quietly abandon him there, Gavin would know

Michael was finished. The pressure was squeezing the life from his chest. Several of his teammates and one reporter had offered their congratulations since he'd hit the locker room. If Michael didn't show, Gavin would take the humiliation as his due, but he had to try. Michael deserved to be publicly claimed. No shame. Gavin hoped all those people from high school had been watching, or—at the very least— heard about their engagement on the news tonight. Michael deserved for Gavin to go that far and even beyond. Still, it had been the biggest risk of his life. Not to mention, his dad would fucking freak.

For the thousandth time since the game ended, Gavin's gaze shot to the mouth of the dressing room. A lone figure leaned against the wall outside the door. With his hands shoved in his pockets, Michael stared at the floor. Gavin would know the top of that head anywhere. His nervousness doubled. Too late, Gavin realized just because Michael had shown didn't mean they weren't still over. His feet still moved in the man's direction, because that was where Gavin belonged. At his approach, Michael's chin lifted. Their gazes met. A burning sensation began at the backs of Gavin's eyes. Nothing else had ever mattered to him the way Michael did. For years, he'd lived in some fucked up form of stasis, waiting for this moment right here. His feet didn't stop until his body collided with Michael's. Their mouths met halfway. The rest of the world ceased to exist. Gavin couldn't stop touching Michael. The man's kiss tasted a lot like forgiveness.

Gavin pulled away only far enough to touch his forehead to Michael's. Still, he couldn't stop stroking the man's face. He'd been so damn scared he'd never get to touch him again. "I love you. Thank god you showed up." Gavin didn't care if he rambled. For days, everything had felt wrong without Michael. He couldn't imagine the rest of his life like that.

"I love you too. Where else would I be?"

Gavin laughed at the question but didn't loosen his hold on Michael. "Anywhere, I suppose."

Michael shook his head, squishing their foreheads together as he did. "You're the love of my life. This is where I belong. I'm sorry for everything," Michael tacked on, surprising Gavin. "You deserve better from me than I acted."

Gavin leaned away, unsure of what to say. Not only had he not expected Michael to apologize, Gavin wasn't sure Michael owed him an apology, especially since Gavin had been pretty damn high handed tonight and they hadn't discussed that yet.

"Come home with me tonight."

Michael nodded. "I'd like that, since I'm your fiancé and all."

A smile exploded across Gavin's face. "Come home with me," Gavin repeated. "I think I can convince you stay for good."

"Is that really what you want?"

"Do you want to talk about it here?" Gavin shot back as quickly.

"You're right," Michael said, straightening away from the wall. "I'd never make you get on your knees here." Michael turned away as he made the claim, stealing Gavin's chance to see if he meant the words. It sounded a hell of a lot like Michael wasn't turning him down.

Hope spurred Gavin forward, following on Michael's heels and overcoming him. He wrapped his arms around Michael's waist from behind and matched his steps as they headed for the door. "So, it's like that, huh? You plan to make me beg."

"Not beg," Michael said, sounding happy. "Just ask properly instead of assuming. Plus, I have a point to make."

That last bit confused Gavin. "Okay. What's that?"

"You'll see."

That sounded ominous. All Gavin could do was pick up his pace and try to get home as fast as possible. The sooner they were alone, the faster Gavin could celebrate his victory. On the drive home,

Gavin waffled between racing to the house and driving as slow as possible. Even though Michael acted like they were okay, Gavin was terrified it was a temporary reprieve.

"Did you tell Marshall you were leaving with me?"

Michael snorted. "Marshall ditched me five minutes after the Jumbotron incident."

Gavin's shot a quick glance Michael's way. "What? Why would he do that?"

"It's a long story," Michael said. He ran his hand up Gavin's thigh. "I'll tell you all about it later."

Since Gavin's house came into view, he let it slide. They had bigger issues right now than Michael's flake of a brother. Not to mention, as self-absorbed as Marshall might be, he loved Michael and would always have his back. Whatever happened, Gavin was certain it wasn't too huge of a deal. "Damn, looks like I left half the lights in the house on. I guess I was a little nervous when I headed out earlier."

"You? Nervous? I can't picture it," Michael said as he opened his door without waiting for Gavin.

Gavin jumped out after him. Maybe Michael wouldn't always let him play the gentleman, but that didn't mean he would let Michael walk to the door without holding his hand. The sensation of Michael's palm pressed against his was one the things he'd missed the most this past week. Gavin shook his head at the thought. He couldn't believe it had only been a week since Michael's birthday. It had been the longest goddamn week of his life. As they walked hand in hand to the front door, Gavin tried calculating how many seconds there were in a week, because he'd damned sure felt every single one go by. He unlocked the door and waved Michael inside ahead of him. The moment he stepped through the door, Gavin's feet froze to the floor. His gaze moved around the room before landing on Michael. Michael chewed his bottom lip and stared at Gavin looking more frightened than Gavin had ever seen him.

"Your stuff is here," Gavin said for lack of anything else. Truly, he didn't know how else to react.

Michael nodded. "Not all of it. The movers only had so much time, and we haven't really talked about whose furniture we'd use... or if we'd use furniture at all," Michael finished lamely. "But I needed to make a point," Michael said, coming back to life, as if he realized he wasn't making the most of the moment. "You see, you think I don't know you, but I do. I might've been a weird kid, but this weird kid somehow snagged you," Michael said, sounding determined and proud. "You cheated your way through calculus, and no one noticed when you took art as an elective, but I did. I noticed all those things. Maybe you kissed Marshall, but you're mine.

You've always belonged to me. In the past six years, I don't know how many other men you've met, and I don't want to know. All I do know is—in the past six years, I've only dated one person and I canceled more dates with him than I went on, because I knew you'd be back. Don't ask me how I knew, but I did, because I fucking know you. I know you're dark and obsessive and when you care, you do it with everything. Even if I didn't admit it to myself, I knew you'd find your way back, because you are *mine* and I am *yours*. If you think moving my furniture in unannounced is insane, walk away from me again, and I'll show you crazy."

Gavin couldn't breathe past the love choking him. There were too many thoughts running through his mind at once. They'd both shown just how far they'd go tonight. He hated to up the game by tackling Michael to the floor and fucking the man until he couldn't walk. Gavin tried taking a few breaths instead. He cast a desperate look around the room, trying to focus on anything other than his need to claim the other half of himself. His gaze landed on the wall above the sofa. The two paintings he'd given Michael hung there.

"I had a few others framed for the bedroom," Michael said, sounding entirely too calm for a man who was about to get fucked hard. "I should admit, I also stole the sketch book from the car and had those framed for your studio."

Gavin closed the front door.

"Of course, I don't know if those are up yet. Like I said, there wasn't much time."

Gavin toed off his shoes.

"If you don't want me here, I'll move everything out," Michael said, still rambling.

"Shut up, Michael."

"Okay." Michael pressed his lips together, as if emphasizing his point. He lasted all of ten seconds. "Just let me say one more thing—I just want to be with you. If you want to live together or not. If you want to get married or—"

"Shut up, Michael," Gavin repeated.

Michael went back to pressing his lips together.

"We're getting married on Monday." Michael opened his mouth, as if to interrupt, but Gavin held up his hand, stopping him. "It's not your turn to speak," Gavin reminded him. "You spoke your piece already. First thing Monday morning, we're getting married. I have to be honest, I don't really know the laws about waiting periods or whatnot, but it's happening even if we have to catch a flight to somewhere else. I should've run away with you when you made the suggestion years ago, but I didn't. But now, this back and forth is over, you understand?"

Michael didn't respond.

"I'm not hearing anything reassuring from you," Gavin said, feeling his temper slip.

"You told me to shut up," Michael reminded him. "More than once, actually."

It was getting harder by the minute to keep from smiling or tossing Michael to the floor. "You can speak as long you're telling me what I want to hear."

"Monday morning works for me."

"We're keeping the bean bag for my studio, so you can play games while I paint."

Michael visibly fought back a smile. "I say we buy more than one. We need one for our bedroom."

Gavin had to clench his fists behind this back to stop himself from reaching out for Michael, but he wasn't finished yet. "Speaking of gaming, you'll also reactivate your account. I can't believe you'd delete all your hard work just to avoid speaking to me."

"I didn't delete my account," Michael said. He pulled his phone from his pocket. "I changed my username. Come see," he said, motioning Gavin closer. He handed his phone to Gavin. "See? That's me now."

Gavin stared at Michael's new username. He tried not to smile, but he couldn't stop himself. "Propertyof#1HatTrick," Gavin read aloud.

"It was a moment of weakness and wishful thinking."

He couldn't take it any longer. Gavin handed the device back to Michael before digging the ring box from his pocket. He dropped to one knee because he'd promised himself he would. Because Michael deserved to be asked properly no matter how many times he'd already accepted. He stared up into the face of the man who'd stolen his heart years ago and never let it go. "Michael Vaughn Frost, you're the only man I've ever loved and I can't live without you. Would you do me the honor of marrying me?"

In spite of already agreeing, Michael visibly swallowed, as if this was the first he'd heard of the idea. He didn't look at the ring. His gaze never wavered from Gavin's. When Michael answered, his voice broke. "A million times if you'd let me."

Gavin shifted to his feet and calmly slipped the ring onto Michael's finger. He wanted to celebrate and scream his triumph at the top of his lungs. Instead, he slowly drew Michael closer while holding the man's gaze. All his plans to win Michael had finally come to fruition. If Michael had any idea how long Gavin had that ring, he'd run for his life.

"I need to marry you fast, before you realize how insane I am over you," Gavin admitted before he could stop himself.

Michael's mouth turned up in the corners and a wicked glint entered his eyes as he encircled Gavin's neck. "You weren't listening earlier. I know exactly how crazy you are for me, and I love it. How could anyone else ever be enough after you? No one else would go as far to be with me. Give me all your insanity. I want it."

Something inside Gavin snapped. He snatched Michael off his feet and slung him over his shoulder. Peals of laughter reverberated off the walls of his house, making it feel like a home for the first time ever. Gavin headed for the bedroom. Michael felt up his ass as Gavin made his way down the hall. A laugh caught in his throat.

"Damn, I love your ass. Are you wearing underwear?" Michael asked. He tugged at the waistband of Gavin's jeans, as if trying to check for himself.

Gavin laughed harder. Michael always knew how to calm his most intense moments of obsession when his mind threatened to boil over. Inside the bedroom, he set Michael on his feet, ensuring the man's body slid down his so Michael could feel how hard Gavin was for him. "I should've spent every day telling you how much I love you."

Michael toyed with Gavin's t-shirt. "You've shown me and that's better." As Michael made the claim, he shoved Gavin's shirt up until Gavin raised his arms. When Gavin's eyes were covered by the material and he couldn't see, Michael captured his lips just as he'd done in Shreveport. Gavin froze, savoring the moment. He took his time tossing the shirt aside. If Michael wanted to be in control, Gavin didn't have a problem with that. He stood still, waiting to see what Michael would do next. Michael's hands slid down his chest and stomach, leaving a trail of goosebumps behind. Each breath Gavin took came harder than the last. Michael's gaze never left his. He looked so damn serious and intense, Gavin couldn't look away even if he wanted.

He popped the button on Gavin's jeans. "You know I wouldn't have let you walk away from me, right?"

Gavin didn't respond. His throat wouldn't work. Looking at Michael now was like looking in mirror. It was the first time he'd noticed Michael looked at him with the same insane glint.

Michael slid Gavin's zipper down. "I'll never let you go."

If Gavin had ever been more turned on, he couldn't remember it. In fact, he worried he might blow in his jeans before Michael could set his erection free. Then, Michael's hand dipped inside Gavin's underwear. A pant escaped Gavin with enough force it made his chest ache. Michael cupped his cock and stroked. Gavin had to lock his knees to keep from going down. He didn't even blink as he stared at Michael. The man's lips were slightly parted and his eyes looked unfocused. A flush rode high on his cheeks. As Gavin looked on, white teeth sank into Michael's bottom lip. Gavin snapped. His mouth collided with Michael's hard enough he tasted blood. He tore at Michael's clothes. Something ripped. He didn't care. Whatever it was, he'd replace it. Michael would never want for a thing as long as Gavin lived.

Air left his lungs on a whoosh as his back hit the mattress. Gavin stared up at the ceiling. It took him a moment to realize Michael had shoved him down. He didn't have time to adjust to his new circumstances before Michael straddled his hips. Reality was blurred. Clothes disappeared and lube coated his naked cock. Before he had time to mentally prepare, Michael's hot asshole engulfed him. A shout escaped him. Michael's mouth covered his, swallowing the sound. He might've been embarrassed by the lightning fast orgasm if Michael's cum wasn't coating his stomach and chest. He didn't know what happened. It was if they exploded into some sort of pleasure-filled inferno. Gavin couldn't catch his breath. His body jerked with each wave of ecstasy. It was like little tiny bolts of electricity on his dick.

Pulse after pulse of pleasure rocked him, and then Michael lifted, impaling himself on Gavin's cock once more and another orgasm slammed into him, shocking him. He'd never had multiple orgasms in his life. He thought they were a myth. With his head thrown back, Gavin gasped for air. He'd never been more scared of having a heart attack.

In his fear, he cried out for Michael. "Michael." Even he heard the pleading in his voice. Michael's mouth covered his with the lightest of pressure. Everything righted itself and slowed. He took his first steady breath. Michael's tongue brushed his. Gavin took another breath. His fingers dug into Michael's back, anchoring him to reality. "I love you," Gavin whispered as he changed angles and deepened their kiss. He couldn't say it enough to soothe his heart.

Michael shifted positions and cuddled as close to Gavin as possible. "I love you too, baby. Could we stay right here where you can hold me for the rest of the night?"

He hadn't even needed to ask. Gavin wasn't sure he'd ever move again. He had the love of his life in his arms. Gavin didn't need anything else to survive.

CHAPTER TEN

A seventy-two-hour waiting period required by the state of Louisiana had Michael and Gavin getting married on the beach in Key West. For as long as Michael lived, he knew he'd never forget the way Gavin stared at him as he repeated his wedding vows. He didn't know how he'd missed the pride in the man's eyes, as if Michael was the greatest thing in Gavin's life. Michael's chest hadn't stopped aching since. A new weight of responsibility bore down on him, making it hard for him to breathe. He didn't regret marrying Gavin. That was the best decision of his life. He was afraid of himself. Coach was due to arrive any minute, and Michael was ready to crawl out of his fucking skin. Gavin had spent years hiding his real self because of his father and although Gavin never talked about it, Michael got the impression Coach wasn't handling having a gay son well. Michael was scared he might beat the shit out of the man if he said the wrong thing. He might be a little guy, but he had protective rage on his side. Coach might've given Gavin life, but that life now belonged to Michael. No one hurt his husband. The only thing currently saving Coach from Michael's wrath was Gavin's confession. Coach was the only person in Gavin's family still speaking to him since coming out. Michael's heart broke every time he thought about it.

Michael made one more pass through the house, ensuring it was clean enough for visitors. They'd stayed at Gavin's for two weeks before Mara had shown up with a brightly wrapped wedding present—the deed to the rental house where Michael had been living. They were still moving things around, trying to decide where everything would go. Gavin's house was now empty and on the market. Between the money from the sale of his house and the money Gavin made from working on the movie set, he had the funds for his art studio. Gavin hadn't decided yet when he'd get started. For now, they were enjoying their newlywed status.

The doorbell rang, and Michael's heart raced up into this throat. He shot a glance Gavin's way. He looked fine—like it was any other day. Michael moved to answer. When the door swung wide, he blinked in surprise at the crowd of people on the other side. Mara had one arm linked through Coach's while Coach stared down at her with stars in his eyes. Cal stood at their backs with a baby carrier linked over each arm.

Mara's eyes and smile were bright. "Look who I ran into in the drive. He was nice enough to walk me to the door."

Michael checked Cal's reaction. A small smile hovered on the man's lips, as if unsurprised by anything when it came to Mara. "Coach has always been a gentleman," Michael said as he stepped back, making room for their visitors to come through the door.

Coach's gaze never left Mara as they filed inside. "You never told me your husband was friends with this lovely woman," Coach said when Michael closed the door behind him.

"Michael is more than a friend," Mara said, her smile somehow managing to become even brighter. "I couldn't survive without him. He's like family. I'm thrilled he's married your son. They're perfect for each other."

Coach nodded, as if every word coming from Mara was gospel. "I completely agree. This is the first chance I've had to visit since they ran away to get married, screwing me out of being part of the wedding," Coach said, flashing his first disapproving glance their way. He immediately went back to staring at Mara as he led her to the couch. She didn't release his arm until she got settled.

Mara released an irritated-sounding sigh. "I wasn't thrilled about that either, especially since I was pregnant at the time and couldn't travel. Otherwise, I would've tracked them down and invited myself."

Coach filled the empty spot beside her as if Mara's husband wasn't there. Cal shot Michael an amused glance. Michael relieved him of one of the baby carriers. He moved the blanket covering it aside to see which baby he held. Bright gray eyes stared out at him. Michael barely stopped himself from gushing. He'd never spent much time around babies until Mara had given birth. Now he had a hard time staying away from the pair. Michael tuned out the rest of the room as he unbuckled Lucas. The boys were identical in almost every way, but Michael could tell them apart. Lucas had a small birthmark on his chin. Logan didn't. It wasn't until he settled the tiny warmth against his chest and leaned back in the chair to cuddle with the bundle that he noticed how quiet the room was. He tore his gaze away from Lucas long enough to look up. Every eye was focused upon him.

He got the feeling he'd missed something important while he'd been focused on one half of his greatest baby loves.

"What?"

"You look like you need a baby in your arms," Gavin said, making Michael's heart turn over in his chest. He sounded like he enjoyed the thought.

"I've always wanted grandkids," Coach said, adding his thoughts.

They hadn't talked about a family. Now that Michael had the idea in his head, it felt right. His throat swelled as he stared at his husband. Was this the same person who'd shattered him into a million pieces once upon a time? Michael couldn't remember the pain anymore. Gavin had filled him with so much beauty and light Michael couldn't see anything else. Their life would be amazing because he knew Gavin wouldn't allow it to be any other way.

"See," Mara said, dragging Michael's attention away from the greatest love of his life. "It's like I said outside, they look at each other like no one else exists. I've never seen two people more meant for each other."

"I see that," Coach said, sounding thoughtful.

Michael's gaze slid back Gavin's way. One day soon, he'd have to find a way to thank Mara for being the most amazing person on the planet. Right now,

Michael couldn't see anything other than the happily ever after sitting across from him.

The End.

Keep an eye out for the next Hard Hit book, *Bang*.

Charity Parkerson is an award winning and multi-published author with several companies. Born with no filter from her brain to her mouth, she decided to take this odd quirk and insert it in her characters.

*Seven-time Readers' Favorite Award Winner

*2015 Passionate Plume Award Finalist

*2013 Reviewers' Choice Award Winner

*2012 ARRA Finalist for Favorite Paranormal Romance

*Five-time winner of The Mistress of the Darkpath

Connect with her online:

--Join my street team: facebook.com/TeamCharityParkerson

--Sign up for my newsletter: http://bit.ly/CharityNews

--Website: charityparkerson.com

--Facebook: facebook.com/authorCharityParkerson

facebook.com/TheMenofSin

--Twitter: twitter.com/CharityParkerso

❀ Created with Vellum